That terrifying ripping sound . . .

The wave lifted her again, and once again heaved her onto the rock, which now had long needles like a cactus, needles that pierced her torn wet suit and pierced her skin. . . .

Frantically she tore at the suit. She had to pull it off.

She struggled free of it at last and tossed it into the churning ocean. She was in her bathing suit now. She looked toward the beach. She could see her beach umbrella sticking up in the sand. The beach umbrella had been cut to shreds.

How did that happen? Who did that?

And then the wave returned, lifted her high, and slammed her against the rock. . . .

That sound again, that terrifying ripping sound. This time it wasn't her suit being slashed. It was her skin.

**Other Point paperbacks
you will enjoy:**

Blind Date
by R.L. Stine

The Baby-sitter
by R.L. Stine

Final Exam
by A. Bates

Trick or Treat
by Richie Tankersley Cusick

My Secret Admirer
by Carol Ellis

Funhouse
by Diane Hoh

Prom Dress
by Lael Littke

point

BEACH PARTY

R.L. Stine

SCHOLASTIC INC.
New York Toronto London Auckland Sydney

ISBN 0-590-43278-8

12 11 10 9 8 7 6 5   1 2 3 4 5/9

Printed in the U.S.A.   01
First Scholastic printing, August 1990

BEACH PARTY

Chapter 1

Karen Mandell drove the way she did everything else in life — foot down hard on the gas, full speed ahead, never look behind. The gray morning haze was lifting, and a hot, white sun came burning through as Karen squealed around the curve, roared past a line of slow-moving cars and vans, and slipped her navy-blue Mustang convertible into a narrow space in Lot C at LAX.

Before climbing out of the car, she stopped to examine herself in the rearview mirror and straighten the blue, sleeveless T-shirt she wore over white tennis shorts.

I look okay, she thought. Not as pretty as Ann-Marie, but okay.

Karen's oval face was framed by straight, black hair that rested comfortably on her shoulders. She had dark skin that always looked tan, and shocking blue eyes, shocking because they were so wide, so blue, and so unexpected. They were eyes that belonged on a fair-skinned blonde. On Karen's dark face beneath her black eyebrows, they looked so dramatic, so mysterious, it was impossible not to stare into them.

She smoothed her hair, jumped out of the car, searching for some way to remember this parking spot, and hurried to meet Ann-Marie.

"Good timing!" Karen cried. Ann-Marie was just coming out of the gate as Karen arrived. Dressed in hip-hugging designer jeans and a heavy brown sweater, she was carrying a large, red canvas bag and a tennis racket. She dropped everything when she saw Karen, and the two friends rushed forward with beaming smiles to hug each other.

"Putting on a little weight, aren't you?" Karen said, stepping back. It was a running joke. Ann-Marie was as thin as ever. She looked like a fashion model with her slight figure, her straight blonde hair cut fashionably short, her emerald eyes, and her high cheekbones and pale, creamy skin.

"Don't mention weight," Ann-Marie groaned, picking up her bag, which appeared to weigh as much as she did. "They served the worst meal on the plane."

"What was it?"

"I'm not sure. It was bright yellow, burning hot on the outside and frozen solid on the inside."

"Must have been lasagna," Karen said. "How did it taste?"

Ann-Marie rolled her eyes. "Fabulous. I had to have seconds." They followed the signs to the baggage pickup. "I can't believe I'm here, Karen." They walked past a large window. "Oh, look. The sky is yellow from all the pollution. I guess I *can* believe I'm here!"

Karen looked at her watch. "You've been here fifteen seconds, and you've already put down L.A."

"That's a record for me," Ann-Marie said, shifting the red bag to her other hand, and dropping the tennis racket. "I must be slowing down."

Karen laughed. "I'm just so glad to see you." She flung an arm around Ann-Marie, forgetting the weight of the canvas bag, and nearly knocked her over. "Oops. Hey — what have you got in there — presents for me, I hope?"

"Nope. I brought Sandy." She shook the bag and called into it, "Hold still in there, Sandy." Then she looked back at Karen. "He insisted on coming. He's madly in love with you, you know."

"How *is* your little brother?" Karen asked, laughing.

"Compared to what?" Ann-Marie joked. "Compared to Freddy Krueger, he's okay, I guess. He's at that sarcastic age. You know. Everything you say to him, he's got a sarcastic remark."

"Aw, he'll grow out of it," Karen assured her.

"He *will*? I never did!"

They went down an escalator and followed the signs down another endless corridor. Suddenly Ann-Marie stopped. "Karen — what's that around your neck?"

"This?" Karen's hand went up to the crystal she wore on a chain.

"Oh, no. I *knew* it," Ann-Marie wailed. "Get me

back on the plane. I can't stand it out here. That's a crystal, right? You do weird things with crystals, right? You think they have magic powers, and you talk to them and — "

"Stop! Come on, stop!" Karen protested. "I just wear it because it's pretty," Karen said, not meaning to sound quite so defensive.

"For sure," Ann-Marie said. "Like gag me with a spoon."

"Ann-Marie, nobody says that anymore. Not even valley girls," Karen said, making a face. "Actually, Mike gave me this crystal, before I broke up with him."

"I know. I know. The astrology counselor at school told you to break up with Mike, right?"

"Hey — you really *haven't* outgrown your sarcastic phase," Karen said. "Breaking up with Mike was really a bummer, you know."

Ann-Marie apologized quickly, her cheeks coloring. "Sorry. It always takes me a while to lose my New York edge. Really. I'm sorry. I — I just feel like such an alien out here. Like I'm from Mars or something."

"No problem." Karen gave her a warm smile. "I think you'll feel right at home in a little while. Wait till you see where we're staying."

They stopped in front of the baggage conveyor belt. Ann-Marie dropped her bag to the floor and placed the tennis racket on top of it. Two small yellow cases were going round and around, looking very lonesome on the long, winding belt.

"You mean we're not staying at your house?" Ann-Marie asked.

"In Westwood Village? No way."

"Then where?"

"It's a surprise." Karen gave her a mysterious smile.

"Say — how's your mom doing?" Ann-Marie asked.

"Pretty good. It took her a while, after the divorce. I mean, I think she took it a lot more personally than Daddy."

"Divorce is pretty personal," Ann-Marie cracked.

"You know what I mean. Anyway, it took her a while to get going again. I mean, she was like a zombie for months. She'd sit around playing her old Beatles records and cry."

"That's too bad. But she's better now?"

"Yeah. A little. I think she went out on a date last week. Some guy who sells real estate in the valley."

"And your dad?"

Karen shrugged. "He's definitely weirded out."

"Huh?"

"He's driving a red Corvette, for one thing. And he's blow-drying his hair."

"Weird."

"Actually, I don't see him that much. Of course, I never did. He bought me a car. A Mustang convertible. Do you believe it?"

"Is that good?" Ann-Marie asked, not being sarcastic.

"Yeah. It's what you might call an awesome car."

"You might. I wouldn't. I don't drive."

"You don't drive? You're seventeen, and you don't drive?" Karen looked positively shocked.

"No. I take the subway, usually. It's a lot faster."

"The subway? Don't you get mugged and killed if you take the subway?"

"Not everyone," Ann-Marie said, staring past Karen as more suitcases began to magically appear on the conveyor belt.

About fifteen minutes later, they were out in the hazy sunshine looking for where Karen had parked the car. "This *is* an awesome car," Ann-Marie said when they finally found it. "I love the white leather seats. How do you keep them clean?" Karen helped her load her suitcase and bag into the trunk.

"Daddy got me a new wet suit and new skis, too," Karen said, sliding behind the wheel. The seat was hot against the back of her legs.

"He buys you a lot of presents, huh?"

"Yeah. He's definitely trying to buy my love. And you know what? It's working!"

Both girls laughed as Karen backed out. It took a while — even for Karen — to get out of the vast airport. Then Karen headed the car northwest along Lincoln Boulevard. The bright sun had burned away most of the haze, and the air was getting warmer.

"Where are we going?" Ann-Marie asked.

Karen shook her head mysteriously. "You'll see." They squealed to a stop because of some construction up ahead. "Hey — I've been doing all the talking. What's new with you? Did you have a good year?"

Ann-Marie looked away. "Not really."

Karen was more than a little surprised. Ann-Marie was flip and sarcastic, but she always had a lot of enthusiasm. "How come?"

"I don't know. It was sort of a wasted year, I guess. It's hard to explain. My high school is so big, and — well, everyone's so immature. I — "

"And how's Clay?"

"I meant to write — I broke up with Clay. Or maybe he broke up with me. I'm not sure." Her normally pale face was bright crimson.

"Gee, I'm sorry."

"Me, too," Ann-Marie said in a near-whisper. Then she added wistfully, "Maybe it isn't all over. Everything was sort of up in the air when I left."

Karen could see that Ann-Marie was really upset. She and Clay had been going together for two years. Karen wondered what had happened. She probably would never find out. Ann-Marie seldom liked talking about herself.

The girls had been friends since about the age of nine, growing up as neighbors in Westwood Village. When they had started high school, the friendship had seen some hard times. In fact, Ann-Marie didn't speak to Karen for six months after Karen started to date a boy Ann-Marie was interested in.

"You're always making me jealous of you," Ann-Marie had said one day during an angry exchange. And Karen had never forgotten it. It seemed such a sad, revealing thing to say.

But then, Ann-Marie had moved with her family to New York, and the friendship was revived through letters. The anger, the jealousy, the hurt feelings seemed to dissolve over the miles.

Now Ann-Marie was back in L.A. for the first time since she'd moved, and Karen was so happy to see her, she thought she might burst.

The traffic started moving again. "Good old Highway 1," Ann-Marie said, forcing a smile. "Yeah, it's great to be back."

It was nearly an hour later when they pulled up to the low, three-story gray shingled apartment building. "Here we are," Karen said, squeezing the Mustang into a narrow parking space. "What do you think?"

"Speedway?" Ann-Marie asked, reading the street sign. "Where are we?"

"Venice." Karen started to roll the top up.

"Venice? You mean the place with all the weirdos and the roller skaters?"

Karen grinned. "Wait till you see the apartment."

"Whose apartment?"

"Ours. Well, actually, my dad's." Karen locked up the car and walked around to open the trunk.

"Your dad has an apartment in Venice?"

"I told you he's weirded out. He's even rented this apartment right across from the beach. He's having a second adolescence, I guess. I think he wants to bring back the sixties. I mean, he's got psychedelic posters on the walls — and you should see his girlfriend."

"Girlfriend?" Ann-Marie looked positively appalled.

"Yeah. She looks almost old enough to be my younger sister."

"Wow."

Karen laughed. "You're not from California anymore, Ann-Marie. You're not allowed to say wow."

"Wow. Is your dad's girlfriend staying with us, too?"

"No. They're both gone. They went to some spa in the Springs. The apartment is all ours until the weekend. Daddy won't be back until late on Saturday. Isn't this great? Our own apartment right across from the beach!"

Karen helped Ann-Marie lug her suitcase out of the trunk. Ann-Marie looked up uncertainly at the low, gray building, which looked more like a motel than an apartment house.

"Your mom was always so strict," Ann-Marie said, carrying her bag and following Karen up the steps. "I can't believe she's letting us stay here on our own — even for a few days."

"She doesn't know," Karen said, her blue eyes glowing.

"Huh?"

"She thinks Daddy is here with us. I didn't tell her he was going away. It's our little secret."

"But, Karen — " Ann-Marie hung back. "Do you really think this is such a good idea?"

Karen unlocked the door and pushed it open. She tossed Ann-Marie's bag in, then stood back to let her friend inside the apartment first. "Of course it is," Karen said, with a mischievous smile. "What could happen?"

Chapter 2

"The beach is so beautiful at night," Karen said, kicking off her sandals and stepping into the cool sand.

"It — it's not very crowded," Ann-Marie said, looking around warily.

"People don't know what they're missing," Karen said, ignoring her friend's reluctance. "Come on. What's there to be afraid of? When's the last time you smelled the Pacific?"

"Two years, I guess," Ann-Marie said, stepping off the boardwalk and following her friend onto the beach. "Hey — wait up. Do you always have to walk so fast?"

"You're the New Yorker," Karen called back, not slowing her stride. "You're supposed to be used to a fast pace."

"No one could get used to you," Ann-Marie said, jogging to catch up. She heard a noise behind her and turned to see two boys in T-shirts and black spandex bicycle shorts roller-skating at full speed down the boardwalk. "Aren't they cold?" she asked

Karen, shivering. The air grew cooler as they approached the water. The wet sand felt clammy under her bare feet.

"It's a little chilly," Karen admitted. "But who cares? Here we are, Ann-Marie. It's summer, and you're back, and we're on the beach, and we're going to have nonstop fun for the next month!"

"When does the nonstop fun begin?" Ann-Marie grumbled.

"Come on. Just look around," Karen enthused, refusing to acknowledge her friend's sarcasm.

Ann-Marie had to admit that it was a beautiful night. The sun had just fallen, and the sky was pale evening purple, with tiny white dots of stars beginning to pop out and sparkle. The steady, rhythmic rush of the low waves, splashing lightly on the smooth shore, drowned out all other sounds. Against the darkening sky, the water was as blue as an afternoon sky. It sparkled and shone, as if holding the sunlight, refusing to allow the light to slip away.

"Pretty," Ann-Marie said, smiling at Karen. They walked silently along the shore. The water seemed to grow darker with every step they took.

Ann-Marie shivered and wrapped her arms around herself. She was wearing cutoffs and a light wool poncho, but the cold ocean air made her wish she'd worn something heavier. She couldn't believe Karen, who was wearing short shorts and a T-shirt and didn't seem the least bit cold. "Wow. I feel a long way from home," she said quietly.

"Ann-Marie, you lived here in L.A. most of your

life," Karen reminded her, bending down to pick up a shell, then quickly tossing it into the water.

"But I guess two years is a long time. It all seems so different." She turned and looked back at the boardwalk, also known as Ocean Front Walk, which was dark and nearly deserted. The shops had all closed before sunset. The summer season, with its influx of tourists and young people and crazies from all over, hadn't really begun. The Venice Pavilion across from Market Street stood dark and deserted, a low concrete bunker covered with graffiti.

Karen dug her feet deep into the wet sand. "Oh, that feels so good! I love it!" she shouted happily. She lifted her face toward the water to better feel the cold spray. "It's really good for your skin," she told Ann-Marie.

"Too salty," her friend grumbled. "Listen, I'm freezing to death. Could we go back and get changed?"

"Yeah. I guess." Karen couldn't hide her disappointment that Ann-Marie wasn't being more adventurous, more enthusiastic.

"Where is everyone, anyway?" Ann-Marie asked, pulling her light poncho tighter around her shoulders.

"Main Street mostly. That's where everyone in Venice goes at night."

"Aren't there parties on the beach or anything?"

"No. Most people are kind of afraid," Karen admitted reluctantly.

"Afraid? Of what? Afraid of the dark?"

"Oh, you know. Gangs, I guess."

"Oh."

Karen began jogging toward the boardwalk, her bare feet slapping the wet sand. Ann-Marie followed close behind. "Hey — where did we leave our shoes?"

"Up this way, I think," Karen called back to her. "Just past the Pavilion."

It was very dark now. The purples and grays of the night sky had darkened to black, broken only by tiny pinpoints of white starlight. The ocean behind them was even darker than the sky.

They located their sandals and were slipping them onto their wet, sandy feet when the five boys appeared, five tall shadows that seemed to materialize like dark, grinning ghosts.

They wore denim and leather, angry-looking T-shirts with the names of heavy metal groups emblazoned across the fronts, visible even in the dim light. Their hair was short and spiked, or scraggly, down to their shoulders. A couple of them had diamond studs in one ear. They all wore the same amused expression.

They're trying so hard to look dangerous, Karen thought.

The five of them shuffled closer, sneakers scraping against the asphalt of the boardwalk, their hands in their jeans pockets or jammed into the pockets of their open jackets.

Karen was the first to speak. "Hey — how's it goin'?"

This seemed to strike some of them funny. They laughed, short, high-pitched laughter.

"Real fine," one of them said. He was tall and lanky with short, blond hair, spiked straight up. His smile revealed two deep dimples on his narrow cheeks.

He's kind of cute, Karen thought.

He raised his hand to scratch his jaw, and Karen could make out a tattoo of an eight ball on the back of his wrist.

Karen thought she recognized him from school. His name was Vince Something-or-other. He had bumped into her once in the hallway, causing her to drop all her books. When he'd stooped to help her pick them up, he'd seemed very embarrassed. She remembered he hadn't said a word.

"How are *you* doing?" one of Vince's friends, a tall, dark-haired boy with a serious skin problem, asked, leering at the two girls. He took a deep drag from the cigarette between his lips, then tossed it onto the asphalt and stamped it out beneath the toe of his black boot.

"We were just leaving," Ann-Marie said, pulling Karen's arm.

"Hey, it's early," one of the boys said, moving to block their way.

"Yeah. We just got here," the dark-haired one said, staring hard at Ann-Marie.

Karen glanced at Vince, who hadn't said anything. He was standing back, a few feet from his buddies, his face expressionless.

"You guys better not go for a swim," Karen said. "You forgot your rubber ducky inner tubes."

They all laughed sarcastic, phony laughs, everyone except Vince, who stood frozen, watching silently.

"We heard there was going to be a party," the dark-haired one said, looking Ann-Marie up and down. "Isn't that right, Vince?"

Vince shrugged in reply.

"Yeah. A beach party," one of the others said, nervously fiddling with the zipper of his denim jacket.

"Have fun, guys," Karen said, starting to walk past them.

"Hey, wait. You're invited."

"Yeah. In fact, you're the party," the tall one said, his voice filled with menace.

Karen caught Vince's eye. He quickly looked away. He swept a large hand back through his close-cropped hair, his face twisted in a frown.

He looks a little like Sting, Karen thought.

"Isn't it past your bedtime, boys?" Karen asked. "You don't want your mommies to worry about you, do you?"

"You can tuck me in anytime," one of them said.

They all laughed and slapped each other high fives. This time, Vince got into the act, too.

"Come on — let's go," Ann-Marie whispered to Karen.

Karen nodded and tried to step past two of them who looked enough alike to be twin brothers, but they moved to block her path. "Which one do you want, Vince?" one of the twins called.

"He wants *you*," Karen cracked to the twin who had asked the question.

"I like the one with the mouth," Vince said softly.

"Which one do *you* like?" Karen asked Ann-Marie loudly, ignoring Vince.

"I — just want to go," Ann-Marie said, looking very scared.

"I like the one with the brain," Karen said. "Which one of you is using the brain tonight?"

This time, no one laughed.

"Hey, we're not bad guys," Vince said, staring into Karen's eyes. He took a couple of steps toward her, his hands in his jacket pockets.

"Not bad compared to *what*?" Karen snapped.

He didn't smile. His dark eyes burned into hers.

The five boys formed a loose circle around Karen and Ann-Marie.

"Are you going to let us go?" Karen demanded.

No one replied.

Ann-Marie gripped Karen's arm. Her hand was freezing cold.

The circle tightened as the silent boys moved in on them.

Chapter 3

"Hey — what's going on?"

"Whoa!"

The circle opened wide as Vince and his buddies turned to see who was calling out to them.

Two boys stood on the boardwalk, one carrying a skateboard. The other one, tall and powerfully built, wearing jeans and a dark-hooded sweatshirt, stepped forward, taking long, confident strides.

"Hey, you girls — I've been looking all over for you," he said, ignoring the five startled-looking boys.

"Huh?" Karen stared at the boy as he approached. I've never seen him before in my life, she thought.

"Yeah. We thought you were going to wait with the others," the other boy said in a hoarse, scratchy voice. He was wearing a white windbreaker, which flapped noisily in the wind.

"Sorry," Karen said, catching on quickly. "We were looking for you." She glanced at Ann-Marie to make sure her friend understood what was happening.

Ann-Marie looked frightened and totally confused. The wind off the ocean had blown her short, blonde hair straight back. She looked like a little girl, a frightened little girl.

"Well, come on. We're late," the tall boy said impatiently. He grabbed Karen's hand and began to pull her away. "You coming or not?"

Vince and his friends had watched this scene in startled silence. But now Vince moved quickly to block their way. "Hold it right there, buddy," he said in a low, menacing growl.

"My name's Jerry, not Buddy."

Vince smiled for some reason, a thin, slow smile that revealed the deep dimples in his cheeks. "Well, Jerry," he said slowly, "where you going with our girlfriends?"

Vince's buddies all laughed at this and closed ranks behind the two girls.

We're caught in the middle, Karen thought. This could get pretty ugly.

"Girlfriends?" Jerry looked Vince up and down. His friend moved quickly to his side. "Hold on a minute, man," Jerry said. "You're talking about my sister." He motioned to Karen.

Vince sneered. "She's your sister?"

We *do* look a little alike, Karen thought, looking closely at Jerry. He had straight, dark hair like hers, and light eyes, and a perfect, straight nose.

Vince took a step back.

Karen took that as a good sign.

Jerry is bigger than Vince, she realized. Jerry probably works out. He has such powerful-looking arms, such a broad chest. His friend looked as if he was in pretty good shape, too.

"If she's *your* sister, I don't want her," Vince cracked, holding up his hands as if surrendering, and stepping back onto the sand.

"Yeah, she's contaminated!" one of Vince's buddies shouted.

"Don't touch her, Vince. You don't know where she's been!"

They all laughed, except for Vince, who seemed to be thinking hard.

He's backing down, Karen thought. He's going to let us go.

To her surprise, she felt a little disappointed. Not disappointed that a fight had been avoided, but disappointed that she had to leave Vince. She realized that she was attracted to him, the way she was always attracted to danger, to excitement, the way she often was driven to pursue things she knew might not be good for her.

Vince was staring into Karen's eyes. "We didn't mean any harm," he said to her quietly. "Just messing around."

He gave Jerry a threatening look, then turned quickly and motioned for his friends to follow him. They walked off down the boardwalk quickly, laughing about something, slapping each other on the shoulders.

"That was close," Ann-Marie said, sighing. She looked pale in the dim light, but very relieved.

"Where'd you come from, anyway?" Karen asked Jerry.

"Marty left his skateboard over by the rec center this afternoon. We went back to look for it and saw you and your friends."

"They weren't exactly friendly," Ann-Marie said, looking down the dark boardwalk as if expecting Vince and his friends to return.

"No. They were *too* friendly," Karen corrected her. She turned to Jerry. "Listen, it was really nice of you to rescue us."

"Yeah, it was, wasn't it!" Marty said. "I sort of couldn't believe it myself. It was Jerry's idea, really. He's into being macho."

"And what are you into?" Jerry asked Marty.

"I'm into running away!" Marty replied. His windbreaker flapped in the strong breeze. He grabbed at it, trying to pull it tighter, but it flapped out of his grasp. He had curly, brown hair over a round face, small, black eyes and round puffs of cheeks.

He looks like a squirrel, Karen thought. A fat little squirrel storing up nuts for winter. Jerry, on the other hand, was a great-looking guy. A little too straight, too preppy for her taste, maybe. But she might be able to make an exception this time — especially since he had rescued her from those toughs.

"It's kind of cold, don't you think?" Ann-Marie said, looking toward the houses across from the beach.

"Yeah. Let's get warmed up," Jerry said, rubbing his hands together. He looked at Karen. "You two have plans?"

"No," Karen answered quickly. "We were just going for a walk and — "

"Well, do you know RayJay's on Main Street? A bunch of us sort of hang out there. It's not a bad place — "

"We've got to get changed first," Ann-Marie said.

"Yeah. Right," Karen agreed. "We'll meet you there. RayJay's. I think I know where it is. On Main Street near Park?"

"Don't meet us. We'll walk you home and wait for you," Jerry said, giving her a warm smile.

"Okay. Sounds good," Karen said, returning his smile. "And it'll be our treat — since you were so brave."

"Well, you're pretty brave to be seen with *us*," Marty said in his hoarse, scratchy voice, and then laughed as if he'd made a truly hilarious joke.

RayJay's was a small, bustling coffee shop and pizza restaurant in the basement of a two-story house on Main Street between Park and Brooks. Karen found a parking place a few doors past the restaurant, parked the Mustang, and cut the engine.

"It's only a few blocks from the apartment," Ann-Marie protested. "We could've walked."

Marty looked at her curiously from his position beside her in the backseat. "Walk? What's *that*? You're not from around here, are you!"

"Some people out here don't walk to the bathroom," Karen joked.

They climbed out of the car and looked up and down Main Street, which was crowded with people window-shopping, on their way to dinner, or to the many clubs and bars that lined the narrow street.

"Looks like Greenwich Village," Ann-Marie said. "Only everyone looks a lot healthier."

"Don't let looks fool you," Karen said. She hopped down the concrete stairs to the open entrance of RayJay's, the others following behind.

The restaurant was a long, low rectangle with two rows of red vinyl booths going straight back to a mirrored back wall. A rainbow-colored jukebox beside the bar against the near wall was playing a Willie Nelson record. Two waitresses scurried back and forth down the wide aisle. They wore long, red aprons over black T-shirts and red short shorts, and little red plastic baseball caps with *RayJay's* in black on the front.

The restaurant was smoky and hot, filled, for the most part, with loud, laughing young people. Karen spotted an empty booth about halfway to the back. She started to lead Ann-Marie and the two boys to it when they were stopped by an angry-looking girl in tight-fitting black slacks and a pale green Esprit sweater.

"Where've you been?" she asked Jerry, pushing past Karen.

"Oh, hi, Renee." Jerry looked at Karen, embarrassed.

Renee was about a foot shorter than Jerry. She

had a pretty, oval face with big, dark brown eyes, and piles of frizzy brown hair that she swept straight back and kept in place with a long, pearl-white hairband.

"Where were you?" she repeated. She had a high-pitched voice. Karen thought she sounded like a little mouse. "Stephanie and I have been waiting forever."

"Well . . ." Jerry's face grew bright crimson. He gestured to Karen and Ann-Marie.

Renee looked at them suspiciously. "Hi," she said, and quickly turned back to Jerry.

"We met Karen and Ann-Marie," Jerry said. "They were having trouble and — "

"They rescued us," Karen interrupted, jumping right in to help Jerry, who seemed to be very flustered.

"Rescued you from what? From boredom?" Renee snapped.

I don't think I like her, Karen thought.

"These boys were giving us a hard time on the beach." Ann-Marie stepped in. "Jerry and Marty got rid of them for us."

A girl with long blonde hair was waving frantically at them from the first booth near the bar. "Hi, Stephanie," Marty waved back.

"Come on," Jerry said, putting an arm around Renee's shoulders. "We can all squeeze into the booth. Then we'll tell you the whole story."

"It sounds fascinating," Renee said drily. But she allowed Jerry to guide her to the booth. Marty quickly squeezed in next to Stephanie, and Renee and Jerry slid in on the other side. Karen and Ann-Marie were left to sit uncomfortably on the outside edge.

"Don't they have any bigger booths?" Karen complained.

"No. Guys usually only bring *one* date," Renee said pointedly, glaring at Jerry.

"This isn't a date," Karen said quickly. "Jerry said a whole bunch of kids hang out here and — "

"Oh, is *that* what Jerry said?" Renee snapped, her little mouse voice rising.

Karen glanced at Ann-Marie. She wondered if her friend felt as uncomfortable as she did. Jerry could have at least told us that he and Marty already had dates, she thought. From the looks of things, Jerry and Renee and Marty and Stephanie had been couples for quite a while.

"This is my treat," Karen announced, trying to remove some of the tension from around the table. "I promised I'd treat since Jerry and Marty were so brave."

"*Them??*" Both Renee and Stephanie cried in unison.

Everyone laughed.

Karen realized that Jerry was staring at her. He had the nicest smile on his face.

He looks a little like Tom Cruise, Karen decided. She returned his smile, but cut it short when she saw that Renee was watching.

"We already had dinner," Renee said.

"Me, too. But I'm still hungry," Marty said, his arm carelessly around Stephanie's shoulder.

"I'm starving," Karen said, ignoring the dirty looks she was getting from Renee. "How's the pizza here?"

"It's round," Renee said helpfully.

"Sounds good," Karen said. "Let's get a pizza."

"I just want an iced coffee or something," Renee said unhappily.

Jerry continued to smile at Karen. She began to worry that his face was frozen in that position. When he and Marty got up and went to the back of the restaurant to talk to some guys they knew, Karen actually felt a little relieved.

The four girls talked, awkwardly at first, but then more comfortably. Stephanie had a cousin who lived in New Jersey but worked in Manhattan, so she and Ann-Marie found something to talk about. Renee and Karen talked about what a weird place Venice was. Then Renee bragged about her parents' house in Bel Air and about all of the celebrities she'd met because her dad was "in the business."

Karen was grateful when the pizza finally arrived. It meant she could concentrate on eating instead of talking.

The boys returned when they saw the pizza. Karen drifted in and out of the conversation. Her mind wandered back a few hours, back to the deserted boardwalk. She found herself thinking about Vince, about how he tried to look so tough but how those deep dimples of his betrayed him. She tried to recreate the scared feeling she had had back on the dark beach, the creeping feeling of terror when the boys circled them and started to move in, like vultures to their prey. It was scary but thrilling at the same time.

How far would those boys have gone? she wondered.

What would have happened if Jerry and Marty hadn't happened by?

". . . the best beach parties at Malibu," Jerry was saying when Karen's attention drifted back to the table. She looked up and realized that he was talking to her. "You'll have to come sometime," he said. "You, too," he added quickly, looking across the booth at Ann-Marie.

"Sounds like fun," Ann-Marie said, wiping pizza sauce off her chin with a napkin. "Where is this party beach?"

"It's a secret," Jerry told her. "We slide down these cliffs and onto the beach. It's really great. Especially at night."

"Malibu is so beautiful," Ann-Marie said.

"It's pretentious," Renee said, sighing. She didn't bother to amplify her opinion.

"Maybe we'll all go Friday night," Jerry said, doubling his enthusiasm in an attempt to cover for Renee's definite lack of it.

"Maybe," Karen said, grabbing another slice of pizza off the tray.

The rest of the evening went by quickly and pleasantly. Even Renee seemed to pick up and get into a better mood.

It was nearly midnight when they decided to call it a night. "I can drive everyone," Karen offered, stifling a yawn.

"No. I have my car," Renee said, waving a set of BMW keys under Karen's nose.

As they slid out of the booth, Jerry leaned forward and whispered into Karen's ear, "You have great eyes."

She smiled and started to thank him for the compliment, but stopped when she saw Renee watching them from the restaurant doorway. "So does Renee," Karen said pointedly.

Jerry blushed and hurried back to Renee.

As they stepped out of the restaurant into a surprisingly cool evening for June, the street was still filled with people. On the corner an old man wearing a Dodgers cap over sunglasses was seated on an overturned trash can, playing a funky blues tune on a harmonica. Several couples were clustered outside an after-hours club across the street. Car horns honked. The street was still filled with traffic.

Karen had to pay the cashier, so she was the last one out of the restaurant. As she stepped up onto the sidewalk, she was surprised to find Renee waiting for her, the others having gone ahead.

"It's busier now than it was at eight," Karen said, looking down the street.

"Listen, Karen." Renee grabbed Karen's arm. Her hand was cold. Her fingers tightened around Karen's wrist until Karen felt like crying out. "Stay away from Jerry," Renee said in a flat, low tone, pressing her face close to Karen's, so close Karen could feel Renee's breath on the side of her face.

"I really mean it. Stay away from Jerry."

Then Renee let go, and hurried to join the others.

Chapter 4

"Just watch it, man."

"You watch it, man."

The two boys faced each other, their faces alive with anger. Suddenly they both groaned in recognition.

"Not *you* again!"

"You!"

"You following me or something?"

Vince kicked at the sand with a bony foot. Jerry moved his surfboard in front of him like a shield.

They tried to stare each other down, then Vince spoke first without changing his expression. "Hey — you bumped me, man."

"You're a hard guy. You can take it." The slight tremble in Jerry's voice indicated that his heart wasn't entirely in this fight.

"Maybe you should stick to a boogie board," Vince said, staring with distaste at Jerry's green Day-Glo baggies. Vince scratched his neck. Jerry could see the tattoo on the back of his wrist, a small, black eight ball. "Maybe you should go play with your *sister*," Vince said, sneering, balling his big hands into fists.

Vince kicked his own surfboard angrily. "There's a whole ocean out there, man. Why'd you have to bump me?"

"There's no surf anyway," Jerry muttered, feeling a little calmer. Vince obviously didn't want to fight, either. Jerry had never seen Vince without the other members of his gang around. Vince probably felt insecure on his own, Jerry figured. "The undertow is real strong, but there's no surf."

"You gonna give me a weather report, too?" Vince snapped. He kicked at the sand a little harder, sending a wet clump onto Jerry's surfboard.

Jerry took a step back. He stared past Vince, watching the low waves splash onto the shore. Out in the ocean, two white sailboats glided slowly by. He heard laughing voices behind him and turned to see two guys bombing down the boardwalk on unicycles, their arms waving above their heads.

"Just watch it, man. You've got two strikes against you now." Vince ran a hand back through his short, blond hair and shook his head, as if dismissing Jerry from his thoughts. He walked past Jerry, dragging his board behind him, heading to where his gang buddies were waiting on the edge of the beach near the boardwalk.

Two girls in tight, pink bicycle shorts and white midriff tops skateboarded along the blacktop, looking self-consciously sexy. Vince called out something to them as they passed. They laughed but didn't slow down.

Jerry watched them disappear around the curve of the boardwalk, then started back to the blanket. "Hey — what was that all about?" Renee called.

She sat up on the blanket, her skin pink from the sun. She was wearing a small gold bikini. Her frizzy brown hair was tied behind her head with a rubber band.

"So? What's with you and that punk?" she repeated, shielding her eyes with her hand.

"Oh, nothing," Jerry said, sliding beside her on the blanket. "Mmmmm. Coconut." He inhaled deeply. He loved the smell of coconut suntan lotion. "What number are you using, Renee? A hundred and thirty?"

"No. Eight." She didn't laugh at his joke. She never did.

He inhaled again, then licked her arm. "Mmmmmmm. I love coconut!"

She pulled away from him. "Don't get kinky, Jerry." She laughed, finally.

"Yucccch! It tastes terrible!" He pulled up the top of the cooler and pulled out a Coke.

"I didn't know you and Vince were friends," Renee said, lying back down, stretching out until she was comfortable. A large, high cloud rolled over the sun, covering the beach in sudden shadow.

"Vince? Is that his name? We're not friends. He and his gang were the ones who were giving Karen and Ann-Marie a hard time Monday night."

Renee frowned at the sound of Karen's name. "So why were you talking with him?"

"I accidentally bumped him with my board, and he got mad."

"You shouldn't bump him," Renee said, frowning up at the dark cloud. "He's bigger than you."

"Next time I'll bump someone small," Jerry said, sitting up straight, staring out at the water. "Anyway, he decided to let me live this time."

"That's lucky." The cloud rolled on, and the shadow moved down the beach. Renee pulled her sunglasses down from her forehead and over her eyes. "It's lucky the rest of his gang wasn't there. They'd eat you alive."

"Thanks for the vote of confidence."

"They're *bad dudes*," Renee said, laughing for some reason. She had the strangest sense of humor. Jerry never could figure out what she would laugh at and what she wouldn't — or why.

Jerry sat silently for a while, looking around the beach, which was pretty empty considering what a nice day it was. Of course, some schools hadn't let out yet. It was only the second week of June. But still, Jerry thought, the beach and the boardwalk were pretty empty.

"The water's pretty warm for June," he said. "I saw some jellyfish. It's awfully early for jellyfish."

"I'm bored," Renee said, with an exaggerated yawn.

Oh, no. Here we go again, he thought.

This was the way their arguments had been starting lately, with Renee saying she was bored. Bored with what? She usually couldn't say. Jerry began to realize that she most likely was bored with him but was just afraid to come right out and say it.

Was he bored with her? Maybe. He couldn't really decide. He knew he'd been thinking about Karen an awful lot since Monday night. In fact, he'd been thinking about Karen nonstop.

"What do you mean you're bored?" he said, sighing.

"Bored. B-o-r-e-d. Do I have to spell it for you?"

"You just did."

"Being sarcastic doesn't help, Jerry. Being sarcastic is really boring."

"Look, Renee, I really don't want to start with you. Summer has just started. We're here on the beach, and — "

"But it's boring for me to lie here while you're off surfing all afternoon."

"I *wasn't*." He slapped the blanket angrily. She could get him exasperated so quickly these days. "I wasn't surfing. There's no surf. I was just testing the water a bit."

"You were just bouncing into that creep, trying to get yourself killed."

"That's not funny."

"I didn't mean it to be. What am I supposed to do all summer while you're running from Catalina to Malibu with your surfboard? Sit and watch?"

"I thought you were working on your tan, Renee." He knew that was pretty lame the instant he said it. Why did he always say the first thing that popped into his head? It was such a bad habit.

"Oh, that's real stimulating. Working on my tan."

"Well, you brought your wet suit and that new snorkeling gear. Why don't you try it out?"

She sat up and made a face. "I'm too bored."

"You're always bored lately," Jerry said, challenging her to say what was really on her mind, knowing that he was venturing out into dangerous waters, but annoyed enough not to care.

"Yeah. So? I want a little excitement this summer."

"That's why I think you should try surfing."

"That's not the kind of excitement I had in mind." She flashed him a devilish grin, but remembering she was angry, quickly turned it off.

He picked up the suntan lotion, squirted a white blob of it into his palm, reached over, and started to rub it onto her shoulders. Her pink skin felt soft and tender, like a baby's skin. "I wouldn't mind a little excitement, either," he said softly, leaning over to breathe into her ear.

She quickly rolled away from him. "Don't be a pig."

"Hey — " He reached for her, disappointed, insulted. "You didn't think I was a pig the other night in the back of Marty's van."

She angrily picked up the bottle of suntan lotion and heaved it at him. "Don't talk about it like that! You really *are* a pig!"

She started to gather her things together and throw them into her yellow-and-white-striped Giorgio beach bag. "I don't know what your problem is, Jerry. I saw the way you looked at that girl Karen at RayJay's Monday night. And I saw you staring at those two girls on skateboards just now."

"What are you talking about?"

"You were panting, and your tongue was practically down to your knees."

"What do you care?" Jerry snapped. "You just said you were so bored with me."

She grabbed his arm. It wasn't a friendly touch. She was trying to hurt him. "I just said I was bored," she said, pronouncing each word slowly and distinctly. "I didn't say I was bored with *you*." When she let go, his arm was red. "Don't get any funny ideas, Jerry."

He rubbed his arm. "You hurt me."

"I'll do worse than that if I catch you staring at another girl like that."

Her words gave him a sudden chill.

Then she laughed and gave him a playful shove. "Hey — lighten up," she said, shoving him again.

"Renee, listen. Maybe you and I should talk."

"Talk? What about?" She glared at him suspiciously.

"Well, it's just that — "

He was interrupted by a girl's voice calling from several yards down the beach.

"Jerry — hi!"

"Oh, great," Renee muttered sarcastically.

Jerry had quite a different reaction. "Hey!" he called, jumping to his feet and waving.

It was Karen and Ann-Marie.

Chapter 5

"Maybe we shouldn't go over there," Ann-Marie said, trying to hold her friend back.

"Oh, why not?" Karen replied in typical fashion, and strode quickly across the sand, her wet suit under her arm.

Ann-Marie, carrying the heavy beach bag, struggled to catch up. "Maybe they want to be alone," she argued.

But it was too late. Karen was already calling to Jerry, and Jerry had jumped up and was calling back. As Karen and Jerry greeted each other, Ann-Marie caught the look on Renee's face. It was not a happy one.

"Have you been in the water?" Jerry asked them eagerly, as Karen dumped her wet suit on the sand next to Jerry's blanket.

"Just for a little while," Karen told him.

"The water's so warm," Jerry said.

"Warm? I didn't think so!" Ann-Marie cried. "I was frozen."

"That's because you don't have a wet suit," Karen

said. "We've got to get you one today."

"Oh, right. Just what I need," Ann-Marie laughed. "I'll get a lot of wear out of it. It'll look really great on Madison Avenue!"

So far, Renee hadn't said a word. She was lying on her back, her eyes closed under her sunglasses. Karen looked down at her, wondering where she got the gold bathing suit, and remembered the threat Renee had made to her outside the restaurant on Main Street.

Such a strange thing to do. Karen couldn't imagine why Renee would threaten a total stranger. It was almost unreal, like something out of a TV soap. Was she so insecure about hanging onto Jerry?

Maybe Renee *should* be insecure, Karen thought. Karen had been thinking about Jerry ever since Monday night. She couldn't believe her good luck when she spotted him on the beach just now.

Yes, maybe Renee *should* be insecure, Karen thought. Jerry just might be worth fighting for. And Karen was never one to back away from a fight.

"Hey — whose snorkeling gear is that?" Karen asked, seeing the mask and fins on the blanket and hoping they were Jerry's.

"Mine," Renee said, without opening her eyes.

"Do you snorkel? I've always wanted to try," Karen said enthusiastically.

Renee suddenly sat up and looked at her. "Really? You've never tried it?"

"No. Never," Karen told her. "May I?" She walked over and picked up the mask to examine it.

"My parents are taking me to Cozumel in a few

weeks," Renee said. "They scuba, but my ears aren't good for it. So I just snorkel. They brought me this new gear, and I brought it down here to try out, but — "

"You can't see anything in *this* water!" Jerry exclaimed, standing very close to Karen, pretending to examine the mask along with her. "It's so polluted."

"Well, there's a sandbar over by those rocks out there," Renee said pointing. "The water isn't too chopped up there because of the sandbar. You can probably see a little."

"Oh, I'd love to try it!" Karen cried, fitting the mask over her face and fiddling with the snorkel. "Do you think you could teach me sometime?"

"How about right now?" Renee asked, surprising everyone by springing to her feet. "You've got a wet suit, too, right?"

"Yes, but I don't have a mask or fins or a snorkel," Karen said.

Ann-Marie looked at Karen as if she were crazy, as if to say, "Why are you being so friendly with Renee? Isn't it obvious that Renee hates your guts?"

But Karen seldom thought that way. She always plunged right into an activity no matter who or what was involved. If she wanted to try snorkeling, she would try snorkeling.

"Jerry brought some gear — a snorkel and mask," Renee said. She turned to Jerry, who was still standing very close to Karen. "Let her try on your fins."

"I don't think they'll fit," Jerry said, obediently walking around the blanket to get them.

"Karen has really big feet," Renee said. "They'll probably be okay."

That was an obvious dig, but Karen let it pass. She was too excited to be offended by a crack about her feet. Her feet *were* pretty big, anyway, she realized.

She sat down on the blanket and let Jerry help her into the black rubber fins. "Stand up," Renee said. "How do they feel?"

"I think they'll stay on," Karen said, unsteady on the sand in the big flippers, which were heavier than she'd imagined.

"Okay. Let's get into our wet suits and go down to the water," Renee said.

"This is so exciting!" Karen exclaimed, ignoring Ann-Marie's doubtful looks.

"You're going over by the rocks?" Jerry asked Renee, sounding concerned.

"Yeah. It's the only place we might see a fish or two. Don't worry. We'll be careful."

"What do you mean?" Karen asked.

"Well, the current is funny over there," Renee said, pulling on her wet suit. "It's very calm because of the sandbar. But once you get close to the rocks, the current swirls around and gets pretty powerful. If you're not careful, it can push you into the rocks and make it really hard to get back."

Karen looked out at the blue-green water. She found the line of tall, brown rocks Renee was talking about. They jutted out into the ocean like a natural jetty.

"Maybe you shouldn't go out there," Jerry said. Karen finished zipping the wet suit and turned around to look at him. His face was filled with concern. His eyes darted nervously out to the water.

Renee put a hand on his shoulder. "Don't worry. We'll be okay. Really." She was talking to him softly, soothingly. "You and Ann-Marie can watch us from here. It'll be okay."

That's odd, Karen thought. Jerry seems like such an easy-going, relaxed kind of guy. Why did he get so uptight all of a sudden?

"Come on, let's go," Renee said, motioning to Karen to follow her. They walked down toward the water, carrying their masks and fins. The beach was a little more crowded, Karen noticed, sunbathers taking advantage of the really beautiful afternoon. But there was no one in the water.

"Where are all the swimmers?" she asked, catching up to Renee.

"People don't swim here that much," Renee said. "They come for the freak show on the boardwalk or just to chill out and catch some rays."

They sat down at the edge of the water and pulled on their fins. "So the breathing part isn't hard?" Karen asked.

"No. It just takes a little getting used to," Renee said. "I'll show you. Here. Step into the water." She turned around and started to back in. "That's right. Turn around. It's a lot easier to walk backwards in fins when you're stepping in and out of the water."

Karen followed Renee in. She backed up until the lapping waves were a little above her knees. "The waves are breaking in close today," she said.

"Let's swim out past them," Renee suggested. "I think we can still stand out there."

They swam out a few yards to calm, rolling water.

"Now for the mask," Renee said, holding hers in front of her. "Spit into it."

"What?" Karen wasn't sure she'd heard right.

"Spit into it. On the glass. And rub it around with your fingers. It keeps the glass from fogging up."

Karen obediently spit into the mask and rubbed it around as instructed. "You're a good teacher," she told Renee.

Renee ignored the compliment. "Slip the mask on like this." She pulled it carefully over her hair and slid it into place.

Karen watched her adjust the air hose. Then she did the same. Renee showed her how to bite down on the mouthpiece, and how to clear the hose by blowing really hard if water got inside. "Got it?"

"I think so," Karen said, eager to try it out.

"The important thing is to breathe slowly, normally," Renee said. "If you have trouble, if the mask gets water in it or the snorkel slips out or something, just raise your head out of the water and breathe. It's simple."

"Great. Let's go," Karen said.

"And if you have any problem at all, I'll be there," Renee said. "I'll be right with you the whole time." She gave Karen a reassuring smile.

She's not so bad, Karen thought. Maybe she was just nervous Monday night or something. She's actually really nice.

"Ready?" Renee asked, pushing the mouthpiece between her teeth.

"Ready," Karen said.

"Okay. Remember to kick your whole leg," Renee instructed. "Don't bend your knees. And keep your hands down at your sides."

"Got it," Karen said. This might be a little more complicated than she had thought. Oh, well, too late to back down now. Besides, this was exciting. There was nothing Karen liked better than trying something new for the very first time.

The mask was in place. The straps were tight against her head. She adjusted the mouthpiece and blew hard to clear the hose.

Here goes, she thought.

She watched Renee raise her legs, lower her head, and spread out over the water, and she copied her, breathing hard and fast as she first started to float, then remembering to slow down and breathe normally.

The water was dark and cloudy. She could barely see two feet in front of her.

She raised her head out of the water and was surprised to see that Renee had gotten several yards ahead of her. Her head down, Renee was floating quickly over the rolling water, her legs scissoring rhythmically, swimming straight toward the line of tall brown rocks.

Karen lowered her head again, still breathing rapidly and hard, largely from the excitement of this new experience. She kicked faster, the fins pushing her forward, her arms to her sides. She didn't want Renee to get too far ahead.

The water was a little clearer now. To her delight, Karen saw dozens of small, silver-gray fish, minnows probably. Dark tangles of seaweed bobbed and floated just beneath the surface.

Her breathing slowed. She began to get the rhythm, to feel calm and comfortable.

It was so quiet, so peaceful, so hypnotic. She began to see other fish. A large white fish with yellow markings swam right past her mask.

This is amazing, she thought. Why didn't I ever try this before? In clear water, it must be breathtaking, like descending on another world.

She floated along for a while. The water became cloudy again, green like pea soup. Water tickled her face. She realized the mask was leaking.

She pulled her head out of the water and lowered her legs, allowing the current to take her. Pulling down the mask, she emptied it, then looked for Renee.

Where was she?

Karen had a momentary shock of panic until she realized that she was no longer facing the rocks. She was facing the beach. She must have gotten turned around while watching the fish. With her face in the water, it was so hard to keep track of where she was going.

She spun herself around and was relieved to see Renee just a few yards ahead of her, floating slowly now, her head down, her legs moving smoothly, rhythmically.

She's getting awfully close to the rocks, Karen thought. But I guess she knows what she's doing.

Karen looked back to the shore. They had swum out pretty far. The sunbathers were small dots of color on the yellow strip of beach. Beyond the beach, the boardwalk was just a blur. She wondered if Jerry and Ann-Marie were watching.

Eager to see more, she pulled the mask back up, adjusted the mouthpiece, and ducked her face in once again. She moved toward Renee, and the water cleared as she floated, revealing more and more of its colorful, silent inhabitants.

Renee was right, Karen thought. You can see better here. The water isn't thick and churned up.

A bright blue fish swam up to her, seemed to stare into her mask, then sped away. What an amazing color, she thought. You never see that shade of blue out of the water.

The water felt warmer now. She moved forward, the only sound the steady whoosh of her breath through the hose.

Suddenly she felt a jolt, as if she were being pushed.

She ignored it, but another one followed, a little harder, propelling her forward.

She raised her head out of the water. To her shock, a large rock loomed right in front of her. A wall of smooth, brown rocks jutted before her. She spit out the mouthpiece and turned to find Renee.

"Hey!"

The current was surprisingly strong. It was pushing her, forcing her toward the rocks.

I've gone too far, she thought.

I'm too close.

Where's Renee?

She turned and started to swim away from the rocks. But she was lifted high, as if riding on a wave, and thrown crashing back.

Frightened, she tore off the mask, letting it hang around her neck, and tried swimming again.

But again the current pushed her back.

"Hey! Ouch!"

She was slammed into the side of the rock. Her shoulder hit hard. She bounced off, the pain running down her arm.

I've got to get away from here. I've got to swim, got to move!

"Renee!" she shouted.

Another thrust of the powerful current sent her slamming against the rock again.

"Hey!"

A jagged shard of rock tore through her wet suit. Water poured in, so cold, such a shock.

She was really frightened now.

Where was Renee?

There. She saw her. Renee was only a few yards away, back from the rocks, back from the treacherous current. She was floating tranquilly, her face in the water, the snorkel standing straight up.

"Renee! Help!"

Renee kept floating, her legs kicking slowly.

"Ouch!" Karen slammed hard into the rock.

"Renee — please!"

I know Renee can hear me, Karen thought. She's only a dozen yards away. How can she not hear me? How can she not see me?

"Renee! Help me!"

The freezing water filled her suit, weighing her down. Karen struggled to swim. But her shoulder ached. She couldn't make any headway against the powerful, swirling current.

"Renee — can't you hear me?! Renee!"

She watched Renee paddle along, not lifting her head.

She's ignoring me.

"Renee!" Karen screamed as the current battered her, shoved her against the jutting rocks.

Renee didn't react, didn't look up, didn't turn around.

She did this to me. Deliberately.

She led me out here. She led me to the rocks.

She can hear me. She *has* to be hearing me.

She's deliberately ignoring me.

"Ouch!" Karen couldn't help but cry out as she hit hard against solid rock again.

I'm not going to make it. I can't get out of this current.

She looked up at the rock. Maybe she could climb onto it. Maybe she'd be safe up there.

She reached for it just as the current slammed her forward, and her head hit the rock.

"Got to hang on," she told herself, feeling dizzy, forcing herself not to give in to it.

She tried for the rock again. But it was too slippery. She slid right off.

"Renee — hear me! Please! Renee! Don't leave me here!" she cried.

But the gray-suited figure didn't respond, just kept paddling peacefully, slowly along.

"Renee!"

She hears me, Karen thought. Her terror began to fill her body as the cold waters filled her wet suit.

She hears me. She's not going to look up.

She's waiting there. Enjoying this.

Waiting for me to drown.

Chapter 6

"It's Karen!" Ann-Marie cried. "Look — it's Karen! Up against the rocks!"

"Huh?" Jerry leaped to his feet and, shielding his eyes with his hand, peered out at the line of brown rocks.

"No! Karen! Karen! Karen!"

With the sound of Ann-Marie's terrified cries in his ears, Jerry ran toward the water, kicking up a spray of sand behind him. He hit the water without slowing down, ran several steps, and then plunged into an onrushing wave.

The water was cold, much colder than when he'd been in earlier.

He shuddered and forced himself to keep moving, stretching his arms out in rapid strokes. He could still hear Ann-Marie shrieking, calling Karen's name over and over, even though she was far behind him now.

Where is Renee? he asked himself. Why isn't she helping? Is she in trouble, too?

Jerry was a strong, confident swimmer. But the

shock of the cold water and the horror of the situation had thrown him off stride. The current, he found, was tricky, swirling first in one direction, then pulling him hard in the other.

What happened out there anyway? he wondered. How did Renee let Karen get so close to the rocks?

Where is Renee??

He kicked hard and tried to lengthen his strokes. He couldn't see the struggling girl, but he knew she was somewhere on the rocks straight ahead of him.

"Karen! Karen! Karen!"

He heard Ann-Marie's cry, repeating in his mind, repeating with each stroke.

"Karen! Karen! Karen!"

The name carried on the wind, carried over the water.

I'm coming, Karen, he thought, his chest aching, his biceps tightening. I'm coming, Karen. Hold on. Please hold on.

"Renee — where are you?"

He thought he saw a gray figure, a snorkeling tube. Was that Renee?

Jerry's right leg was cramping up. He stopped kicking for a while and let his arms do the work.

There she is!

He could see the red stripe on the hood of her wet suit.

Are you okay?

Are you conscious?

Let me see your face.

The red stripe disappeared in the swirling water.

It reappeared a few seconds later. What was that bright glare?

It took him a while to figure out it was the sunlight reflecting off the snorkeling mask around her neck.

Hold on. Hold on, Karen. I'm almost there.

He felt as if his lungs would burst. His leg was still cramped, but he kicked through the pain.

"Hey — Jerry!"

It was Renee, calling to him.

She pulled down her mask. She looked very surprised.

"Jerry — what are you doing here?"

"Karen!" he sputtered. He was breathing too hard to talk.

Renee looked confused for a second, and then she must've seen Karen, seen her body battering against the dark rock.

"Oh, no!" she cried. Her mouth dropped open. Her face filled with horror. She swallowed some water, started to choke.

"Renee — are you okay?"

"Why didn't she call me?" Renee cried. "Why didn't she signal or something?"

They both swam toward the rock. Jerry reached it a few seconds later. "Hey — can you hear me?"

Karen didn't reply. Her eyes were closed.

Has she just passed out or something?

Remembering his lifesaving class, he turned her onto her back and put his arms around her.

"Hey — " Renee, breathing loudly, arrived. "Is she okay?"

"I can't tell. She's passed out or something," Jerry said, shivering from the cold. "Look — her suit is ripped."

"Let me help," Renee said. "I can't believe it. I thought she was right behind me."

Jerry was grateful for the help. The current was so strong and so strange. "I've got a leg cramp."

"Let's get out of here," Renee said, grabbing onto Karen from the other side.

They started to pull her back toward the shore. Jerry could see a whole crowd of people at the shoreline. "Come on!" It seemed to be taking forever. It *was* taking forever. The current was trying to force them back, back to the rocks.

"Hope she's okay," Jerry said. "Wish she'd move. Wish she'd talk to us."

It seemed like hours later when they dragged Karen onto the sand.

"Is she okay?"

"Is she alive?"

Anxious voices. The crowd rushed around them, curious, frightened, excited. Jerry and Renee quickly got Karen on her back. They pulled off the hood of the wet suit.

"Get back! Get back!" Renee cried angrily, waving people back.

"Is she alive?"

"Is she moving?"

Jerry, still breathing hard, unable to catch his breath, unable to stop shivering, bent over Karen.

"Get back! Everybody, step back!" Renee

shouted, pulling back the hood of her suit, her frizzy hair matted down against her head.

Suddenly Ann-Marie came running through the crowd and flung herself down next to Jerry. She lifted Karen's head. "Karen? Karen?"

"No, don't — " Jerry started.

"She's dead!" Ann-Marie screamed. "I don't believe it! She's dead!"

Chapter 7

"No!" Jerry cried.

He shoved Ann-Marie away. Then he bent over Karen and pushed hard on her rib cage. He pushed again. Then again. Brackish water spurted from Karen's open mouth.

Jerry kept pushing, rhythmically, the way he'd learned in lifesaving class. The crowd, the voices, the beach, the entire world seemed to disappear as he worked.

Come on, Karen. Come on. Open your eyes, Karen. Breathe. Breathe. You can do it.

He pressed again. Again.

She groaned. More water dribbled from her mouth.

And again.

She opened her eyes.

The voices, the people started to come back. She could hear the roar of the ocean again. She could hear someone crying a few feet behind him. She could see Renee looking on anxiously, chewing on her lower lip, still in her wet suit and fins.

"She's alive!"

"She's breathing!"

The voices were happy now, relieved.

"What's going on?" Karen asked, looking dazed. She started to sit up.

Jerry restrained her. "Are you sure you're ready to sit up?"

"Yeah. Of course."

"She's okay!" Renee cried happily.

Ann-Marie was at Karen's side now. She took Karen's hand and squeezed it, staring at Karen as if she were a ghost come back to the living.

Which maybe she was.

"Uh-oh," Karen said, looking around. "This crowd — because of me?"

"Yes. We thought you had drowned," Ann-Marie told her, looking greatly relieved.

"Renee helped me pull you in," Jerry said, his arm around Karen.

"Renee?" Karen looked up at her.

"Why didn't you call me for help?" Renee asked heatedly, before Karen could say anything. "Why didn't you let me know you were in trouble?"

Karen stared at her in disbelief. Was Renee telling the truth? Had she been too far away to hear Karen's desperate cries?

No, Karen thought. She *had* to hear me. She *had* to.

But there were tears in Renee's eyes.

Was she faking them? Was she putting on a show now so no one would suspect what she had tried to do to Karen?

Two Venice policemen, in dark blue shorts and T-shirts, pushed their way through the circle of on-lookers. "What's going on here?"

Renee pointed at Karen, who was still sitting beside Jerry on the sand. "A girl almost drowned."

The policemen moved forward to talk to Karen. "What happened?" one of them asked her.

Karen's hair was tangled and wet, the back covered with sand. She looked as pale as cake flour, but her blue eyes were regaining their lively sparkle. She sat up, propping her hands behind her in the sand.

"I got too close to the rocks. The current got me. I couldn't get back," she told the policemen.

One of them picked up her snorkeling mask and examined it. "Why were you snorkeling there?" the policeman asked suspiciously, handing the mask back to Karen.

"You can't see anything there," his partner added.

"I know," Karen explained. "I never snorkeled before. Renee said she'd show me how. I just wanted to try it."

The policeman turned back to Renee. "You Renee?"

Renee nodded.

"You don't give very good lessons," he said drily.

"There's no lifeguard yet," the other policeman said, turning to look up at the empty lifeguard tower.

"I know," Karen said. "Jerry saved me. Jerry and Renee."

Karen started to get up, but her legs felt shaky.

Ann-Marie helped keep her steady, allowing Karen to lean on her arm. "I'm okay. Really," Karen insisted.

"Get going," one of the policemen yelled, shooing the crowd. "Show's over. Come on. Get moving."

"Party time! Who's got beer?" someone yelled.

A few people laughed.

"This isn't the best place to snorkel," one of the policemen said quietly to Karen. "Your friend should've told you that." He eyed Renee suspiciously.

"She didn't call me," Renee said, sounding more angry than upset. "She didn't let me know she was in trouble."

"Glad everything's okay now," the policeman said, and motioned for his partner to follow him back to the boardwalk.

Eventually the crowd dispersed. People returned to their blankets or to the boardwalk, talking excitedly.

"I never swam so fast in my life," Jerry said, catching up to Karen.

"I'm glad you're such a good swimmer," Karen said.

For some reason, his expression changed. His smile faded. A look of horror crossed his face.

"Jerry — are you okay?" Karen asked.

He didn't seem to hear her. He seemed lost in his thoughts, far away. Finally, he snapped out of it. "Sorry. Guess I'm . . . a little in shock."

"You'd better get a towel or something. Aren't you frozen?"

"Yeah. I guess," he said. But he stood beside her, making no move toward his blanket. "You have beautiful eyes," he said.

Karen saw that Renee and Ann-Marie were walking quickly toward them, Renee carrying her fins, looking very unhappy.

"Jerry, really — go get dried off."

But he stood there, staring into her eyes. "Listen, we're . . . uh . . . having a beach party Friday night," he said. He pushed his dark, wet hair back off his forehead. "On that beach in Malibu. A whole bunch of us. Would you like to come?"

"Yeah, I guess," Karen said uncertainly. "You mean Ann-Marie, too?"

"Uh . . . sure. Of course."

"Well, I couldn't say no to anything you asked," Karen said, giving him her widest eyes, turning on the sex appeal. "After all, you saved my life."

Jerry grinned. "Yeah. I did, didn't I. Listen, I can pick you two up. Marty has a van," he said.

"Okay. That'll be great," Karen said. She shivered. "I've got to get out of this wet suit."

"Yeah. Right. Okay. See you tomorrow," Jerry said. "I've got to get dried off, too." He headed back to his blanket.

Karen stood still for a moment, watching him walk over the sand.

Then she turned and saw Renee staring at her, several yards away.

Was that a smile on Renee's face?

The sun was in Karen's eyes. The sand sent up a bright reflection. Karen thought maybe she was imagining it, maybe she was seeing things.

But yes. Renee had the strangest smile on her face. A pleased smile. A triumphant smile.

Karen raised her hand to shield her eyes from the sun.

When she looked back, Renee had turned her back and was heading quickly to the blanket.

"She heard me. I know she did," Karen insisted, later that night. She and Ann-Marie were in pajamas, sitting on the platform bed in her room, eating Heath Bar Crunch ice cream from containers, half-watching a *Cheers* rerun on the TV. A soft breeze off the ocean invaded the room through the open window, cool and salty, making the light curtains billow.

"Karen, I really think you're wrong," Ann-Marie said, biting down on a hard chunk of chocolate. "Renee was underwater, remember. And she had the wet suit hood over her ears. I'm sure she just didn't hear you calling to her."

"I've got to stop thinking about it," Karen said. She stretched back and rested her head on the stack of pillows behind her. The cool breeze felt so refreshing on her skin. "I just can't seem to relax. I mean, she did threaten me, after all. And then she let me get too close to the rocks and — "

"You're starting to sound a little paranoid, if you ask me," Ann-Marie said. "Please — take away this ice cream. I'm going to eat the entire container!"

"Just hold onto it. I'll finish yours after I finish mine," Karen said. They both laughed.

Ann-Marie put the top back on the carton and returned it to the freezer. A few minutes later, she appeared back in the bedroom, fully dressed. "I'm going out for a minute," she called to Karen.

"Huh? What for?"

"To get a carton of milk. I know it's weird, but I always like a glass of milk after ice cream."

"It's weird all right," Karen agreed. But Ann-Marie was already out the door.

She'd only been gone a couple of minutes when the phone rang.

Karen looked at the clock radio on the bedtable. 11:45. Who would be calling this late? Probably anyone. She reached over and picked up the phone.

"Hello?"

Silence.

"Hello?" Karen repeated.

The voice on the other end was a whisper, more like a rush of wind than a voice. "Is this Karen?"

"Yes. I can't hear you very well," Karen said, confused.

"Stay away from Jerry." The words were so soft, as if spoken by a ghost.

"What? What did you say?"

"Stay away from Jerry." This time they were spoken more forcefully in a rasping whisper that hurt Karen's ear.

"Hey — who is this?" she demanded.

Silence.

"Who *is* this?"

And then a click. The dial tone returned.

Karen sat staring at the phone. Finally, she

shrugged and replaced the receiver.

A few minutes later, Ann-Marie returned, carrying a quart of milk in a brown paper bag. She poured herself a tall glass and carried it into the bedroom. "Hey — what's wrong?" she asked, seeing the tense expression on Karen's face.

"I got a call," Karen said. "Someone warning me to stay away from Jerry."

"Huh?"

"That's all they said. I think they were trying to scare me."

"Well, who was it?"

"I don't know. They whispered. You know, disguised their voice."

"Do you think it was Renee?" Ann-Marie tilted the glass back and drank the entire contents.

"Maybe." Karen stared at the window, watching the white curtains blow into the room like ghosts. "I couldn't really tell if it was a boy or a girl. You know who it sounded a little bit like?"

"Who?"

"Mike."

Ann-Marie dropped down into the white leather armchair beside the bed, casually draping her legs over the side. "Mike? Get real! You said you haven't seen Mike in three weeks, not since you broke up with him."

"I thought I saw him yesterday afternoon," Karen said, removing the headband that held her hair in place. She shook her head, and her silky, dark hair tumbled free. "On the boardwalk. I thought I saw him following us. But that's crazy, isn't it? I mean, what would Mike be doing in Venice?"

"Yeah. It's crazy, all right," Ann-Marie agreed. "And why would Mike call you up and whisper for you to stay away from Jerry? He doesn't even *know* Jerry!"

"You're right," Karen said, pulling her hair back, then releasing it, then pulling it back again. "It was Renee. It had to be Renee. She doesn't know me very well, does she?"

Ann-Marie yawned. "What do you mean?"

"I mean, I don't scare easily."

The phone rang again.

Both girls jumped to their feet.

"There she is again," Karen said, frowning. Without hesitating she picked up the phone. "Just leave me alone!" she screamed.

And then her mouth formed a small O of surprise and she nearly dropped the phone.

"Oh. Sorry, Daddy. I thought it was someone else."

Ann-Marie laughed loudly. Karen gestured wildly for her to hush.

"Yes. Fine. Yeah. Okay. Everything's okay. What? Oh. I see." She chatted for a brief while, said good night, and hung up. Then she turned to Ann-Marie. "That was my dad."

"Did he whisper for you to stay away from Jerry?"

"Very funny. No. It turns out that he and his 'friend' " — Karen made two quote marks with her fingers — "have to go on to Tahoe. So he won't be back here for at least another week."

"We're on our own, huh?" Ann-Marie asked, grinning.

"Yeah. We're on our own."

Karen knew she should be as happy about the news as Ann-Marie was. So why did she have this feeling of cold dread in the pit of her stomach?

Chapter 8

On Thursday, Ann-Marie had to visit relatives in Burbank, so Karen decided to spend the morning shopping. Just before lunchtime, she stepped out of a small boutique on Market Street and ran into Mike. He was wearing white tennis shorts and a T-shirt that proclaimed in big green letters: "GUMBY LIVES."

Mike was big with broad shoulders, muscular arms, and a wide neck. He had straight brown hair that he swept straight back off his square forehead, and small, round brown eyes that always seemed to be searching around, looking for something. He reminded Karen of the movie star Jim Belushi, only younger, of course. He even sounded like Jim Belushi.

Karen uttered a little cry of surprise, but Mike didn't seem at all surprised to see her. "Hey, how's it goin'?" he asked, his eyes finding hers, then looking past her.

"Mike — I was just talking about you. What are you doing in Venice?" It didn't come out the way she meant it. It came out sounding slightly suspicious.

"Oh, I got a job," he said, his eyes trailing a blonde wearing a tiny green minidress over dark tights. "On the boardwalk."

"Oh, yeah?" She was still too startled to speak coherently. She had just broken up with him three weeks before. Now here he was following her to Venice.

Oh, get real, Karen, she scolded herself. Mike didn't follow you. This is a total coincidence.

She knew that was the truth, but she only half believed it.

"Yeah. I'm selling T-shirts. Want a Mötley Crüe shirt? Ha ha. I can get you a discount. Ha ha. Pretty boring job. But I get a lot of fresh air, and I'm right on the beach." He grinned at her, the lopsided grin she used to find irresistible. But now she found she could resist it easily.

"Well, that's great, Mike," Karen said, looking both ways for an escape route. "I've got to — "

"What are you doing this summer?" he asked, blocking her path, standing very close to her.

"Well, I'm staying at my dad's place here in Venice. My friend Ann-Marie is visiting from New York."

"Yeah, I know Ann-Marie."

"Oh. Right. Of course you do. Well, she's visiting for a month. Then I'm going away with my mom."

He nodded his head as if agreeing with something she'd said. She realized she also used to find that nod adorable. Now she found it really annoying.

"You've been shopping?" He gestured toward the boutique.

"Just looking around," she said curtly. Why was he dragging this conversation out? Why didn't he just leave?

"You . . . uh . . . seeing anybody?"

"No. Not really."

"So you want to go out or something?" he said, watching a Jaguar pull out of a narrow parking place across the street. "I know this after-hours club on Main Street — "

"Mike, please," Karen groaned. "Give me a break, okay?"

"Huh? What's wrong?" His eyes opened wide and his face filled with innocence.

"You know what's wrong. Everything," she said, desperate to get away. But he was so big, he was blocking the whole sidewalk. "Don't pretend you don't get it. We broke up. In simple English, we broke up." She pronounced the words slowly and distinctly.

"I know, but it's summer now and — "

"And when people break up, that means they don't go out together anymore," Karen continued, talking to him the way she talked to her five-year-old cousin.

He raised his big paw of a hand and rubbed the back of his neck. "Karen, I thought you said you still wanted to be friends. So I took you at your word and — "

"I just said that," Karen said quickly. "I didn't really mean it. That's what you say when you break

64

up with someone. I hope we can stay friends. But no one ever really stays friends. That would be a little awkward, don't you think?"

Why won't he go away? she thought. Just disappear. Poof. Gone. Into thin air. Please. Oh, please. A tiny earthquake. Just big enough for the sidewalk to open under him. No big deal. No tragedy. Just a small, personal earthquake to remove Mike from in front of me.

"I really think we should sit down somewhere and discuss this," Mike said, still rubbing his neck.

"Mike, please — we did all our discussing before school let out. We decided. You weren't having any fun anymore, and I wasn't having any fun anymore."

He reddened. "Don't say that, Karen. We had fun. We had a lot of fun."

"What's the point?" Karen started to lose her temper. "I don't want to go out with you. Can you understand that?" She didn't realize how loudly she was shouting. Across the street, two girls carrying skateboards burst out laughing.

Mike reddened even more, his eyes following the two girls, who turned the corner and disappeared, still giggling.

"Now are you going to get out of my way?" Karen asked, not bothering to hide her annoyance.

"Not until you agree to give me half a chance," Mike insisted, standing his ground.

"Ohh." She felt like slugging him. What was wrong with him, anyway? Didn't he have any pride?

Mike started to say something, but a loud roar

on the street drowned out his words. At first Karen thought the roar was in her ears. She'd been hearing the ocean ever since yesterday afternoon. The roar of the ocean had followed her, even in sleep, as if the waters were calling her back.

But this roar was too loud to be the ocean.

Mike stepped closer to be heard. He was only inches away from her now. She wanted to shove him and run.

But what was that deafening roar?

"Can you hear me?" Mike yelled.

Karen turned to the street, and there was Vince. He was astride a large motorcycle, leaning over the handlebars, grinning at her with those adorable dimples from under his red-and-black helmet, gunning the engine with his black-gloved hands.

"What's going on?" Mike asked, suddenly confused.

"Jump on," Vince yelled, slapping the space on the leather seat behind him.

"Hey — I'm talking to her!" Mike declared angrily.

"Jump on!" Vince repeated, ignoring Mike.

Karen looked at Mike, who was still blocking her path, then at Vince.

Mike reached out for her. She had the feeling he wanted to hold her in place so she couldn't escape.

The motorcycle roared. The sidewalk seemed to shake.

Karen dodged to the side, out of Mike's grasp, pulled herself up onto the back of the big, black-and-chrome motorcycle, and grabbed Vince's leather-jacketed shoulders as he pulled away with an explosion and a powerful jolt.

As they turned right onto Speedway, Karen looked back. Mike hadn't moved. He was staring after them, red-faced, furious.

Vince roared through a stop sign, nearly colliding with two middle-aged women on bikes. The narrow street whirred by in a blur of parked cars and low, white and gray houses.

Where is he taking me? Karen asked herself. What am I doing here? I don't know him. I don't know anyone like him.

The big motorcycle seemed to explode again and with a burst of speed, Vince roared on, heading north toward Santa Monica.

"Hey — stop! Stop!" Karen cried, suddenly regretting her impulsive decision.

But he couldn't — or wouldn't — hear her.

I've made a mistake, Karen thought, gripping his shoulders, leaning against his jacket to get her face out of the onrushing wind.

I've made a terrible mistake.

Chapter 9

He skidded to a stop at the Promenade in Santa Monica, nearly plowing into the back of a Volvo station wagon. A woman dressed in a gray suit, walking a gigantic rottweiler, sneered at Vince and gave him a dirty look. The big, sad-faced dog sniffed at the motorcycle. The woman tugged its leash and pulled it away.

Laughing, Vince slid off the seat and, pulling off his helmet, turned to face Karen. "Ugly dog, huh?"

Karen struggled to arrange her windblown hair, but it was impossible. "You nearly ran it over."

Vince shrugged.

"Why did you stop? What are we doing here?" Karen demanded, still pulling at her hair.

Vince shrugged again. It seemed to be his favorite reply. "Good question."

The day had turned cloudy. A few people were walking along the tree-lined Promenade, but the beach was nearly deserted.

"Well, do you think you could take me back to

Venice?" Karen slid forward on the seat so that she could grip the handlebars.

"I don't know." Vince grinned. He ran a hand back through his short, spiky hair.

"Well, who should we ask?" Karen snapped.

"Hey — " Vince said. She waited for him to continue, but evidently that was his complete statement.

"You know, I really didn't want to come here. I mean . . . ."

"Then why'd you jump on?"

"Mike, that guy back there, he was giving me a hard time, so . . ."

"So here we are in Santa Monica," Vince said, turning away from her to look at the ocean. The waves were high and capped with white foam. The sky grew darker.

"I'd really like to go home," Karen said.

"You're inviting me to your place?" He grinned and leaned forward, bringing his face close to hers.

"Very funny." She pulled back.

He frowned and reached in his jacket pocket for a bent-up pack of cigarettes. He pushed one between his lips and offered the pack to her with a grunt.

"No," she said, pushing them away. "I don't smoke. And neither should you. I mean, what's the point?"

He pulled the cigarette from his mouth. "Yeah. What's the point?" He jammed it back into the pack and shoved the pack back into his pocket. "What's the point?"

"How come you sound so bitter?" Karen said, looking up at the blackening sky.

"How come you sound so nosy?" he asked.

They stared at each other. He was the first to look away. He laughed, a shy, nervous laugh, and kicked at his back tire.

He's really good-looking when he laughs, she thought. "Are you going to take me back?"

"Why don't we keep going?" he suggested, looking out toward the water. "You know. We'll take the Palisades Beach Road."

"It's going to rain," she said.

"You think you're too good for me."

"What?"

"Nothing."

"No. Really. I didn't hear what you said."

"I didn't say anything. Come on. Move back. I'll take you back." He looked really angry. He jumped onto the seat, forcing Karen to slide back. He started the motorcycle with a roar and, without waiting for Karen to get her balance, burst away from the curb, spun around, nearly causing her to topple off, and headed back toward Venice.

"Hey — slow down!" Karen cried, holding onto the shoulders of his leather jacket for dear life.

He immediately sped up, swerved into the left lane to pass a slow-moving van, and nearly collided with an oncoming bus.

"If I want a thrill ride, I'll go to Space Mountain!" Karen shouted.

But he pretended not to hear her and gunned the

motorcycle forward. Karen closed her eyes and held tight.

It started to rain, a drizzle at first and then steady rain. The road became shiny and slick. "Please — slow down!"

He didn't reply. She pressed herself against his leather jacket, wet and fragrant from the rain.

Trees whirred by, a blurred curtain of green and brown, interrupted occasionally by the flashing colors of a billboard. We're not going to make it, Karen thought, as the tires slid noisily around a curve. I'm having a great week — nearly drowned one day, splattered against the highway the next!

Miraculously, a short while later, they were back in Venice, roaring down Speedway, and a short while after that, she was climbing off the seat in front of her apartment building.

The rain had stopped, but her hair and clothes were drenched. Her white sneakers were soaked through and splashed with mud.

"Thanks for the lift, Vince," she said sarcastically.

He didn't look at her, just stared straight ahead. "Say hello to your *brother*," he sneered.

Then he took off without looking back.

Karen stood on the sidewalk and watched him roar around the corner. What was *that* all about? she wondered. Why did he rescue me from Mike? What did he expect me to do with him in Santa Monica? And then why did he get so angry?

He is weird, she decided. He is full-tilt *weird*.

But the wild motorcycle ride, she decided now that she was safely standing on the sidewalk, was kind of exciting. In fact, she wouldn't mind doing it again sometime, sometime when it wasn't raining.

In fact, she decided, she wouldn't mind it if Vince came to rescue her again sometime. All of that shyness, that bitterness, the quiet anger — it was kind of sexy.

Karen, are you losing it totally? she scolded herself. How can you be attracted to a guy like that?

She thought of Jerry and, even though it was foolish, felt somehow unfaithful to him.

Get inside, she ordered herself. That ride has totally scrambled your brain.

Obeying her own command, she hurried into the apartment house to change. The narrow hallway felt hot and damp. She headed to the back where her dad's apartment was — and then stopped.

She took a deep breath.

Someone had painted on the wall.

Black spray paint. The words were scrawled in huge, black letters over the pale green wallpaper.

It started at her door and covered most of the wall to the next apartment.

The paint looked wet. The words appeared to drip down the wall.

They said: *STAY AWAY FROM JERRY*.

Karen reached her hand forward and touched the paint. It felt sticky. She pulled back and saw that her finger was black.

Whoever did this was just here, she thought.

They know where I live.

They were right outside my door.

She had a terrifying thought: Had they been in the apartment, too?

Fumbling with her keys, she unlocked the door and pushed it open an inch. She could see pale gray light pouring through the open window. Cautiously, she pushed the door open wider, took one step into the apartment — and gasped in surprise.

Chapter 10

"Ann-Marie — what are you doing here?"

Ann-Marie hung up the phone, a guilty look on her face. "Oh, hi, Karen. You startled me." She was sitting at the small, glass dining room table, wearing pale blue shorts and a plain white crew-neck top.

"You startled *me*!" Karen said, sinking down across from her on a white vinyl dining room chair. "I didn't expect anyone to be here. I thought you were in Burbank."

"Oh. Well, I changed my mind." Ann-Marie blushed. Her normally pale skin was bright pink. She twisted a strand of her short, blonde hair into a knot. "I wasn't in the mood for my Aunt Freda. Maybe I'll go tomorrow."

"Someone painted on the wall," Karen said, her heart still pounding from the shock of seeing someone in the apartment.

"What?"

"In the hallway. Come look."

Ann-Marie's face filled with confusion. "What do you mean?"

Karen took her hand and pulled her out to the hallway. "Hey — you're all wet," Ann-Marie cried, pulling out of Karen's grasp.

"I was caught in the rain," Karen said.

"It didn't rain here." Ann-Marie gave her a curious look.

"It's a long story. Never mind that. Look." Karen pointed to the words sprayed in black.

"Oh, no." Ann-Marie slumped back against the opposite wall. "Who would do a stupid thing like that?"

"Someone who really wants to frighten me," Karen said, staring hard at the painted words.

"Is it working?" Ann-Marie asked.

That's a strange question, Karen thought, turning her gaze on Ann-Marie.

"Yes. I think it is," Karen said with a shudder.

Chapter 11

"So you left poor Mike standing there on the street and rode off with this gang leader?"

It was Friday night. Ann-Marie had just returned from visiting her relatives in Burbank. Now she was lying on the bed, wearing gray sweatpants and a faded Hard Rock Cafe T-shirt, watching Karen get dressed, very amused by Karen's story.

"He's not a gang leader," Karen said, pulling a purple Esprit sweater over her head. "He just hangs out with some guys."

"Yeah. Some guys who happen to dress alike, just like a gang," Ann-Marie said. "You are unbelievable. You really will do anything."

"I take that as a compliment," Karen said, pulling the sweater down, admiring her figure in the mirror.

"What did you talk about with this guy, anyway?"

"Vince. His name is Vince," Karen said, leaning down to the dressing table mirror to brush her hair. She examined her face as she brushed. The purple sweater made her eyes seem even bluer. "I didn't talk to him about anything."

"Huh?"

"We didn't talk at all. He took me for this wild ride to Santa Monica. Then I told him I wanted to go back, so he turned around and drove back. It was kind of exciting, in a scary sort of way."

"You mean he drives the way he looks?"

"I mean he doesn't stop for anything. And he never slows down, even in the rain."

"Weird. Do you like him?"

"Like him? I don't know. He's terrible. He acts real bitter. He's always sneering, always angry. I think some of it's an act. I can't really tell. Anyway, he's kind of interesting." She grinned at Ann-Marie. "He's certainly different from anyone I know."

Ann-Marie laughed. "That's for sure. What are you going to do if he asks you out?"

Karen's face grew thoughtful, but she didn't say anything. "At least he got me away from Mike," she said finally, sitting down to put on some blusher.

"Mike isn't so bad," Ann-Marie said, stretching.

Karen stared at her friend in the mirror. "Hey — how come you're not getting dressed?"

"I'm not going," Ann-Marie said, lying back on the pillows and stretching.

"What? Why not? It sounds like fun. The beach at Malibu is so pretty at night. You could meet some new kids. Maybe meet a guy."

"I'm too tired," Ann-Marie said, yawning loudly. "Aunt Freda wore me out. She'd wear anyone out with her nonstop talking. Really. She never takes a breath. It was exhausting!"

"Oh, come on," Karen said, disappointed. "You can just chill out on the beach."

"What do you need me for? Jerry will keep you busy enough," Ann-Marie snapped.

She's jealous, Karen thought. I really think she's jealous.

"Jerry already has a girlfriend," Karen said, slipping into blue plastic sandals. "Someone is working very hard not to let me forget that."

"Jerry doesn't seem to remember he has a girlfriend whenever he looks at you," Ann-Marie said.

That's an odd thing to say, Karen thought. What is Ann-Marie's problem, anyway?

"Listen, I just feel too out of it tonight," Ann-Marie said, staring up at the ceiling. "I think I'll just hang around."

"Well, okay," Karen said reluctantly.

A car horn honked down on the street. Karen ran to the window and looked down. A maroon van was parked at the curb. The back door slid open, and Jerry hopped out. He looked up and waved to her. He was wearing tie-dyed jean cutoffs and a black-and-white-striped crew-necked pullover.

He's real cute, Karen thought.

She could see other kids sitting in the van. "Be right down!" she yelled, then realized the window was closed.

"Have a nice time," Ann-Marie said, yawning.

"Yeah. Okay. See you later." Karen took one last glance in the mirror, brushed back a strand of hair from her forehead, and hurried down to the van.

It was a clear, cool evening, more like spring than summer. It'll be cold on the beach, Karen thought.

"How's it goin'?" Jerry asked, helping her into the van. "You know any of these kids?"

Karen peered into the van. "No, I don't," she said, looking around at the smiling faces illuminated by the streetlight.

"You're lucky!" Jerry said, climbing in after her.

"Hey — you know *us*!" Marty called from the driver's seat.

"Hi, Karen," Stephanie called from the passenger seat beside him.

"Oh, hi. I didn't see you up there. Where's Renee?" Karen asked Jerry.

"Yeah. Where's Renee?" a boy in a white sweatshirt shouted in a teasing voice.

"She had to go somewhere with her parents. She's coming later," Jerry said, more than a little uncomfortable. He slid next to her on the seat and pulled the sliding door shut. They were pressed close against each other.

"That's Kenny, Alicia, Normy, and Seth," Jerry said quickly, pointing.

Karen said hi to them, forgetting their names immediately.

"Bring your snorkeling gear?" Jerry joked, as Marty pulled the van away from the curb, turned onto Speedway, and headed north toward Malibu.

"No. I thought I'd leave it home tonight," Karen said, shoving him playfully in the ribs.

Some joke.

"I went snorkeling last week," a boy in the back-seat said.

"Where? In your bathtub?" Stephanie called from the front seat.

"He doesn't take baths," the girl named Alicia cracked in a surprisingly high-pitched, tiny voice.

"How do *you* know?" Marty shouted. Then quickly added, "Don't answer that!" Everyone laughed.

"Hey — are you the girl whose life Jerry saved?" Alicia asked.

"Uh . . . yeah," Karen said, a little surprised by the question. "I was caught on the rocks. Jerry pulled me in."

"Did he give you mouth-to-mouth?" the boy in the backseat asked.

Everyone laughed uproariously.

"Hey, knock it off," Jerry cried angrily. "It was pretty serious, you know."

Everyone obediently stopped laughing.

Then Alicia broke the silence by asking, "Did you have an out-of-body experience?"

"That's kind of personal, isn't it?" Seth joked.

"Shut up, Seth. You're just jealous because no one's interested in your body!" Stephanie joked from the front seat.

Everyone laughed.

"I don't remember anything much at all," Karen answered. "It's all sort of a blank."

"Think you were dead?" Marty asked. "Just for a few seconds, maybe?"

"Only someone who was already brain-dead

would ask that question," Jerry replied angrily. Too angrily, Karen thought. She wondered what was troubling him.

Was he just embarrassed to have been such a hero?

Jerry was pressed tightly against Karen in the seat. He was so warm and solid. She liked being so close to him.

"You're really gross, Marty," Alicia said, shaking her head.

"Thank you, thank you," Marty said, grinning. "What's so terrible? I just asked Karen if she was dead or not. It's not like I asked if she was a virgin or something."

"I don't know," Karen told him.

"You don't know if you're a virgin or not?"

Everyone laughed. Karen felt embarrassed, but she laughed, too. "I mean, I don't know if I was dead or alive. I really don't remember a thing," she said finally.

Suddenly Marty pulled the van off the highway. They began to bump along a narrow dirt road. A short while later, he pulled to the side, stopped, and cut the lights.

"Hey — where are we?" Karen asked Jerry, whispering for some reason.

"We always park here," Jerry explained, pulling open the van door. "It's great. We can slide down the cliffs here. Then we don't have to pay admission to the beach. Or go through anyone's backyard."

Karen hopped down from the van and took a deep breath. The air smelled fresh and salty. She took a few steps and realized they were on the edge of a sloping, dark cliff. The beach spread out below them, illuminated dimly from the highway. Beyond that, she could hear the steady crash of the waves against the shore.

They unpacked the van and tossed blankets and backpacks over the smooth stone cliffside to the sand below. Marty was the first to slide down, wrapping his arms protectively over a big cooler as he slowly dropped. Stephanie followed him, slipping silently down, landing on her knees and getting up quickly to help the next person down.

Karen sat down on the rock edge. It felt cold to the touch. She took a deep breath and pushed herself down. This is great, she thought. Ann-Marie should have come. I wonder why she's been acting so strange, so tense the past couple of days.

Once they were all down on the beach, they spread the blankets in a wide circle on the sand, and then scattered to gather wood for a fire. Surprisingly, it was warmer down on the beach than up on the road. There was no wind at all. Even the spray off the ocean felt unusually warm.

Karen wandered down the shore, looking for firewood. A long, low house, its ocean side built entirely of glass, stood dark and deserted at the edge of the sand, built into the cliffs. Karen picked up a small pine branch, moving closer to the house.

"Hi." The voice right behind her startled her.

"Oh. Hi." It was Jerry. "I didn't see you. It's so dark."

"It's a nice night," he said, his hands stuffed in his pockets.

"Yeah. Look at all the stars," Karen said, tilting her head up. "It's usually so foggy this early in the summer."

"The sand is cold," he said, smiling.

She looked down at his bare feet, wiggling like field mice in the sand. "Your friends are nice," she said.

"Yeah. They're great."

"You know them from school?"

"Mostly."

They had moved into the shadow of the dark house. "I never really got to thank you," Karen said. "You know. For Wednesday."

He leaned his back against the glass wall. Karen moved close to him. Inside the house, she could see toys on the floor, pull toys, some kind of baby rattle. "You don't have to thank me."

"Well, it isn't too often that someone swims out and saves your life. You must be a great swimmer. The current at the rocks was incredible."

"I'm okay. Not great." His expression changed. He looked almost bitter for some reason.

"Well, I think you're great," Karen said, and impulsively, she reached her face up to his and gave him a quick kiss on the cheek.

As she started to back away, she was startled to feel his arms around her waist. He pulled her to him with surprising strength and, holding her so tight she could barely breathe, pushed his lips against hers, pressing harder, harder until the kiss actually hurt.

What's going on? Karen thought. I just meant to give him a peck on the cheek. He seems so . . . desperate. So needy.

She returned his kiss. His hands moved to the back of her head. He pressed her face against his.

This kiss is never going to end, she thought, her heart pounding.

Stay away from Jerry.

The whispered, threatening words on the phone.

Stay away from Jerry.

The spray-painted words scrawled on the wall.

How could she stay away from him? He was so wonderful.

"Stop," she said softly, not wanting to stop, wanting to stop, suddenly terribly confused and conflicted.

He let her go immediately and stepped back, tripping over a small, wooden wheelbarrow.

Karen's lips still throbbed. She could still taste him, still feel him pressing her to him so tightly.

"Hey, sorry," he said quietly, looking toward the camp fire, which blazed orange and red down the beach. He looked very embarrassed. "I'm really sorry. I just — "

"No. Don't," she started. "It was . . . nice." She stepped forward and took his arm. He smiled and seemed very pleased.

"I like you, Karen."

"So I gathered," she teased. She tasted blood on her lips. Such a hard kiss. "I like you, too, Jerry."

They started to walk back to the others, holding hands, not talking.

But Jerry suddenly uttered a low cry and dropped her hand as if it were a bomb.

She saw immediately what had alarmed him.

That figure standing in the shadows of the house.

It was Renee.

She must have seen everything.

Chapter 12

"Hi! Renee!" Jerry tried to be cool, to act as if he were glad to see her there, but his voice was shaky, and he sounded a bit *too* glad.

"Hi, Jerry." She stepped out of the shadows and walked up to them, her hands in the pockets of the cotton windbreaker she was wearing over jeans.

"We were looking for firewood," Karen said. Pretty lame, but at least it was an attempt.

Renee didn't look at Karen, didn't acknowledge her presence in any way. "Nice night," she said, without enthusiasm, and wrapped her arm around Jerry's.

"Yeah. It's great," Jerry said uneasily.

Karen let Jerry and Renee get a little ahead of her. Maybe she didn't see us kissing, she thought. It *was* very dark, after all.

Renee held tightly onto Jerry's arm, leaning against him as they walked over the cold sand to the camp fire. Karen, a few yards behind, couldn't hear what they were saying. But they both seemed to be acting as if nothing had happened, as if Renee hadn't watched them in their long, passionate kiss.

Karen sighed unhappily. She could still taste Jerry's lips on hers. Renee isn't my problem, she told herself, stopping to pick up a large shell that glowed blue in the moonlight. Renee is Jerry's problem.

She watched him walking over the sand, his long legs, his broad shoulders, the way his head dipped when he walked. He was smiling at Renee now. He has such a nice smile, Karen thought. So friendly. It just makes you want to smile, too.

Squeezing the cool shell in her hand, she followed them back to the camp fire. He saved my life, she thought, staring at Jerry. We were meant to be together.

Chill out, she warned herself. One kiss and your brain has turned to oatmeal.

Glowing orange and yellow faces greeted them from around the camp fire. The flickering, bright colors and the twisting shadows made everyone look strange, eerie, like characters in a horror movie.

Karen headed away from Jerry and Renee and settled on a blanket across the camp fire, beside Stephanie and Marty. Someone passed her a basket of sandwiches and a can of Coke. She suddenly realized she was starving. As she ate, she watched Jerry and Renee through the flickering camp fire flames. They seemed to be arguing now, their expressions angry, sitting far apart on the blanket.

Karen tried to join in the conversation with everyone else, but it was hard to concentrate, hard to get Jerry out of her mind, hard not to think about what had happened back at the dark house on the beach.

Suddenly she felt a hand on her shoulder.

"Could I talk to you?" It was Renee, standing above her, her hair orange from the firelight, her face half hidden by shadows.

She looks like a really scary jack-o'-lantern, Karen thought.

Karen peered through the fire at Jerry. He had left the blanket. Where was he? Then she saw him kidding around with two other kids away from the fire.

"Are you coming?" Renee demanded.

"Okay." Karen climbed to her feet quickly.

Renee started walking away from the fire, taking long strides, expecting Karen to follow her. She stopped at the edge of the water and turned around.

As she walked, Karen's mind whirred. What shall I say to her? What is she going to say to me? How shall I play this?

She decided to play it cool.

It's Renee's problem.

It's Jerry's problem.

It's not *my* problem.

It was easy to decide to play it cool. But could she do it?

"I saw you and Jerry," Renee said, without emotion.

At least she doesn't beat around the bush, Karen thought.

Renee waited a few seconds, then when Karen didn't reply, decided to continue. "I tried to warn you Monday night at the restaurant." Her voice was soft. It was hard to hear her over the rush of the waves against the beach. "Remember?"

"Yeah. I remember," Karen said, trying to sound as emotionless as Renee.

What's she going to do? Challenge me to a duel? She was definitely the one who phoned, Karen decided. She was the one who spray-painted the wall. She's that desperate.

Renee's next words startled her. "I tried to warn you because I know you don't understand about Jerry."

"Huh? Understand what?"

Renee waited a while, building the drama. "He needs special care. But you wouldn't know about that, would you?" For the first time, Renee showed a little emotion. Her words were spoken with rising anger.

"I don't know what you mean." Karen bent down and picked up another shell. She rolled it nervously in her hand, staring into Renee's shadowy face, leaning forward to hear her tiny voice over the steady, insistent rush of the ocean.

"You don't know about Jerry's brother Todd? Well, Todd died." Renee watched Karen's face, pleased by Karen's shocked reaction to these words.

"I don't know much about Jerry," Karen said, not sure what she was supposed to say. "We all just met on Monday, remember?"

"Jerry and Todd were very close," Renee continued, ignoring Karen's words. "They were only a year apart. Todd was older. They were swimming.

Last summer. Somewhere off the Palisades. They were both good swimmers, but Jerry was better."

"Yes, he's a great swimmer," Karen interrupted. She knew she didn't want to hear the rest of this story. She thought she knew how it was going to come out. But there was no way to delay it, no way to stop Renee, who continued talking in her tiny voice, as if talking to herself, as if Karen weren't even there.

"There isn't much to tell. They were pretty far out in the ocean. It was the beginning of summer, just like now. There were no lifeguards, few people on the beach. Todd got some sort of leg cramp. He couldn't get back."

"Oh, how awful," Karen muttered. Without realizing it, she was suddenly reliving Wednesday afternoon, was suddenly back in the wet suit, struggling to swim away from the rocks, shouting and signaling desperately for Renee to help her, feeling the panic overwhelm her, feeling the terror freeze every muscle as she crashed into the rocks again, and again, as Renee ignored her pleas, as Renee continued to snorkel.

"Jerry tried to get to Todd in time," Renee continued, looking out at the ocean now. "But he didn't make it."

"You mean — "

"Todd drowned. Jerry watched him go down." Renee was reciting the words in a flat, toneless voice. "Jerry pulled him back to shore, just the way he pulled you yesterday. But he was too late. Too late. Jerry refused to believe it. He kept pushing on Todd's chest, blowing into his mouth. They had to pull Jerry away. He wouldn't let go of his brother. He just refused to accept the fact that his brother was dead."

"Were you . . . were you with him then?" Karen asked, staring out at the black ocean.

"I was with him. It was so terrible," Renee said, her voice catching. She pulled her windbreaker tighter around her. "Jerry felt so guilty. He thought he should have saved Todd. He thought it was his fault. Of course that was crazy. But that's what he thought."

Karen wanted to say something but couldn't think of anything appropriate. It was such a sad, frightening story.

The two girls stood silently staring out into the darkness, listening to the splash of the waves. "Why did you tell me this?" Karen asked finally.

Renee laughed, a strange, inappropriate laugh. Then she turned to Karen and, in a cold, hard voice, said, "I just wanted you to know that Jerry and I have been through some hard times together, and I'm not going to give him up so easily."

The words stung Karen like a spray of salt water. To her surprise, she felt angry. Renee was using the story of Todd's death, using it to threaten Karen, using it to hold onto Jerry.

"That's kind of up to Jerry — isn't it?" she asked, surprised by her own boldness, by the depth of her angry feelings.

Renee didn't say anything. She swept the windbreaker around her shoulders and strode back to the camp fire in a near run.

Karen let herself in silently, carefully clicking the door behind her so as not to wake up Ann-Marie. The hall light was on, the living room dark. The clock by the window said 1:21.

Yawning softly, Karen started to tiptoe past Ann-Marie's room. To her surprise, the door was open and the desk lamp was on.

"Ann-Marie — are you up?" she called, her voice hoarse, probably from the damp ocean air.

No reply.

"Ann-Marie?"

Karen felt weary from head to foot. Every muscle ached as she stepped to the doorway of Ann-Marie's room.

To her surprise, the room was empty. Ann-Marie wasn't there. The bed was still made. Wrinkled shorts and some clean T-shirts and tops were strewn across it.

That's weird, Karen thought. Had Ann-Marie mentioned going out? No. She hadn't.

Earlier, Ann-Marie had said she was tired, too tired to come to the beach party. So where could she be at 1:30 in the morning?

Without thinking about it, Karen picked up Ann-Marie's best silk blouse from the bed. Yawning, she folded it neatly and carried it over to the white dresser.

She shouldn't leave this out, Karen thought.

Ann-Marie had always been so neat. When did she become as sloppy as Karen?

Karen realized maybe she didn't know her old friend as well as she thought she did.

She pulled open the top dresser drawer. It was filled with socks and underwear. She closed it and pulled out the second drawer.

This was the right drawer for blouses and tops. She started to lay the silk blouse into the drawer when something caught her eye.

What's that?

She pushed away some sleeveless T-shirts.

Her hand trembling, she picked up what she had discovered underneath.

It was a can of black spray paint.

Chapter 13

Karen knew it was a dream, but she couldn't get out of it.

She was back in the purple water, in her wet suit and snorkel mask. The water was cold and thick as Jell-O. The air hose seemed to be clogged. She had to push so hard to breathe.

Wake up, she told herself. Wake up out of this nightmare.

She knew that's what it was. But she had to keep swimming, had to keep struggling against the powerful current.

I can't move, she thought. The water is holding me, holding me back.

And suddenly a wave reached up out of the ocean, a wave darker than the waters around it, a wave as tall as a building, and lifted her up. "No!" she cried in the dream. "Put me down! Let me go!"

The jagged, brown rock loomed up like a porpoise leaping from a pool. And the wave sent Karen crashing onto the rock. She hit hard. She could feel the jolt. She could hear her wet suit ripping, a frightening sound, like a lobster being torn apart. She could see the sharp points of the rock shred the suit.

Wake up, wake up!

But the wave lifted her again, and once again heaved her onto the rock, which now had long needles like a cactus, needles that pierced her torn suit and pierced her skin. She cried out as blood began to seep through the holes in the suit, her blood, trickling out through the suit, puddling on the prickly rock.

Frantically she tore at the suit. She had to pull it off. She had to free herself from it.

She struggled free of it at last and tossed it into the churning ocean. She was in her bathing suit now. She looked toward the beach. She could see her beach umbrella sticking up in the sand. The beach umbrella had been cut to shreds. Broken light glinted menacingly off the sunglasses she'd left there.

How did that happen? Who did that?

And then the wave returned, lifted her high, and slammed her onto the rock, which was now much bigger and glowing like a black jewel.

That sound again, that terrifying ripping sound. This time it wasn't her suit being slashed. It was her skin.

She screamed, as she saw her skin tear apart, her side opening up, the bones of her ribs poking out through the gaping hole.

Wake up! Wake up! This dream has got to end!

She tried to stop screaming; she tried to dive into the water. But the wave was too powerful. It heaved her back onto the rock, tearing her skin, splitting it like an envelope being opened, and all her bones were showing now, and the top of her skull, gray as death, poked through her forehead.

And all she could do was scream.

And wake up.

She sat straight up in bed.

Finally. I finally got out of it. I finally woke myself up. It was such a struggle.

Such a struggle just to breathe.

Why am I fighting against the current in my sleep?

She waited for the dream to go away, for the ugly pictures to fade. She waited to forget it, the way she forgot most of her dreams. But it wouldn't go away, not the pictures, nor the sounds, nor the fear.

She could see it all as clearly now as when she was asleep.

And she had the same urge to scream, scream her lungs out at the black sky.

The sheet was hot and soaked with perspiration. She untangled herself from it and kicked it away. She climbed out of bed quickly, hoping to leave the dream behind. But it followed her as she made her way to the closet in the dark and pulled on a light, cotton robe.

The clock said 7:30. Wide awake, still shaky from the vivid nightmare, she walked to the window and pressed her forehead against the cool glass. The sun, still low in the east, was trying to burn through the yellow morning haze.

She stood there for nearly a minute, the dream still replaying in her mind. Then she walked over to the dressing table and saw the can of spray paint. That's where she had left it when she carried it into her room last night.

Ann-Marie. She hadn't heard Ann-Marie come in. Was she there?

Carrying the can of spray paint, Karen stepped out into the dark hallway. Ann-Marie's door was closed. She walked over and silently turned the knob. The door squeaked quietly as she pushed it open. The room was dark. The blinds were closed.

When her eyes adjusted to the darkness, Karen saw that Ann-Marie was sleeping uncovered in the bed, her pajama top tangled at her waist.

How does she sleep without messing her hair up? Karen wondered. That's the advantage of a short hairdo, she decided. She felt her hair with her free hand. It was damp, a tangled mess.

She decided to let Ann-Marie sleep. She didn't really feel like confronting her over the paint can. She wanted to shake the images of the nightmare from her mind before she did anything.

But as Karen turned to leave, Ann-Marie stirred noisily and looked up. "Karen?" Her eyes only half open, her face filled with confusion.

"Sorry," Karen whispered. "Go back to sleep. I didn't mean to wake you."

"What time is it?" Ann-Marie's voice was still choked with sleep.

"It's early. Really. Go back to sleep."

"I got in so late," Ann-Marie said, yawning. She

sat up and rubbed her eyes. Then she stared at Karen. "You okay? You look *terrible*."

"I had a bad dream," Karen said, leaning back against the door. "A really bad dream. Where'd you go last night?"

"Oh. Just out. Main Street."

"I was surprised," Karen said, rolling the paint can between her hands. "You said you were tired and — "

"I don't know. I got bored," Ann-Marie said. "So I went for a walk. I met some kids I knew, and we went to this club on Main Street. It was fun."

"Kids you knew?"

"Yeah. People from school I hadn't seen since I moved east. Did you have a good time with Jerry?"

"Sort of." She *had* until Renee showed up. But she didn't feel like getting into that with Ann-Marie.

"What's that in your hand?" Ann-Marie asked, squinting.

Karen turned on the light. "Don't you recognize it?"

"Huh?"

"I found it in your dresser drawer." Karen moved closer, holding up the can so Ann-Marie could see it better.

Ann-Marie looked very confused. "My dresser drawer? How come you were in my dresser?"

"I was putting something away for you, and I found this."

"A paint can? It isn't mine."

Karen stared hard at her friend, remembering other times, unpleasant times when Ann-Marie's jealousy had made it hard for them to be friends.

"Really," Ann-Marie insisted. "What would I be doing with a can of paint?"

"I think this is the paint that was used on our wall," Karen said, tossing it from hand to hand.

Ann-Marie's mouth dropped open. She held the shocked pose for a short while. "Then how did it get in my dresser? Who put it there? I thought Renee sprayed that message on the wall."

"But Renee hasn't been in this apartment," Karen said, putting the paint can down on Ann-Marie's dresser. "Has she?"

"I don't think so," Ann-Marie said, looking very bewildered. "You don't think that I — "

"No, of course not." Karen decided to deny her suspicions. She realized it was silly to accuse her old friend. Ann-Marie looked genuinely confused, genuinely innocent. Someone had planted that can there. But who? How? "It's such a mystery."

"Really," Ann-Marie said, sliding back onto her pillow, still not totally awake. "What are we going to do today?"

Karen frowned. Was Ann-Marie changing the subject? "I thought we'd hang out at the beach, work on our tans," Karen said, watching her friend.

Ann-Marie groaned. "Another day at the beach? Can't we do something else?"

"I don't get it," Karen said. "If you don't want to spend time on the beach, why'd you come out to L.A.?"

"To see you," Ann-Marie said.

Karen suddenly felt about two inches tall. Ann-

Marie was being a good friend. And what was Karen doing? Suspecting her of doing terrible things, and trying to bully her into spending her time where she didn't want to. With her light hair and fair skin, Ann-Marie had never been a big beach fan. Karen scolded herself for not remembering that.

"I'm sorry," she said. "Maybe we could drive somewhere today. Maybe we could — " But then she remembered. "Oh, no. I forgot."

"What is it?" Ann-Marie asked.

"I made a date with Jerry for this afternoon. To go roller-skating on the boardwalk."

"Oh." Ann-Marie didn't try to hide her disappointment. "I see."

"I'm really sorry — " Karen started. "You could come with us, maybe, and — "

But Ann-Marie interrupted her. "Guess I'll go back to sleep."

She rolled onto her side, her back to Karen. Feeling very guilty, Karen tiptoed out of the room and closed the door.

Karen looked at her watch for about the hundredth time. Jerry was over half an hour late. She was wearing a short pink skirt over black bicycle tights and a white midriff top, and carrying her skates, pacing impatiently back and forth by the spot on the boardwalk where they had agreed to meet.

It was a beautiful, warm Saturday afternoon, the warmest day of the summer so far, and the boardwalk was crowded and noisy. Skaters and skateboarders in skimpy summer outfits rolled by. Boom boxes blared. People crowded the shops. Beyond the T-shirt shop, a woman in a gold sarong with a matching gold bandanna on her head was giving crystal massages, demonstrating the healing power of a large, sparkling crystal. Further down, two lanky high-school boys wearing jeans and matching Def Leppard T-shirts were having their high-tops whitened by a man with a brush and a large bottle of white polish. Kites were flying. A bald-headed dwarf in Day-Glo green baggies was darting back and forth between the shops, offering to let people touch his head for good luck at a dollar a touch.

A typical day on Ocean Front Walk in Venice.

Normally, Karen would have enjoyed the spectacle, the color, the noise, and the sheer nuttiness of it all.

But it was hard to enjoy it when you were wondering if someone was going to show up or not, and worrying about where he could be, and what was taking him so long.

Suddenly someone caught her eye at the T-shirt store. He was standing at a rack of wildly colored shirts, which swayed in the gentle afternoon breeze, and staring back at her.

Mike.

Yes, it was Mike.

As soon as he realized she was looking at him, he turned away, then ducked behind the rack of shirts.

He must be really mad at me, Karen thought.

Well . . . good.

She walked a bit further away from the T-shirt store so she wouldn't have to think about him. Ahead of her, a group of three jugglers were tossing a dozen colored balls into the air. A boy and a girl zoomed past her on unicycles, laughing and holding hands as they zigzagged through the crowd.

Where *is* he?

Karen draped the skates over her shoulder. Is he coming or not? Is he standing me up?

Maybe he's with Renee, she thought, frowning.

What am I doing here, anyway?

Then she saw him hurrying toward her, waving to her and smiling, and she immediately forgot her impatience, her doubts. He was wearing white tennis shorts and a shiny blue, sleeveless T-shirt. His dark hair was blown back, as if he'd been running hard. His skates were flung over his broad shoulders.

He looks gorgeous, she thought.

He caught up to her, dodging a couple of skateboarders, and stopped. "Sorry," he said, out of breath. "I got hung up."

"That's okay," she said. But then, realizing he hadn't given much of an excuse, added, "Hung up?"

"Yeah. I had to see someone." He looked uncomfortable. It was obvious to Karen whom he had to see.

"How's she doing?" Karen asked.

"I don't want to talk about Renee," Jerry said quickly, his face reddening.

"Okay," she replied. There was no reason to pursue the matter. "Want to skate?"

He smiled. "Sure. Come on. I'll race you to the pier!"

The skating date stretched on long after they were tired of skating. They amused themselves on the boardwalk, walking hand in hand, pretending they were sightseers from out of town. They had dinner at a greasy taco stand that advertised an "Amazing Two-For-One Sale," which turned out to be Eat Two, Get One Free. Only, as Jerry pointed out, no one in his right mind would eat two of them!

Then, as the flamingo-pink sun began to descend, they sat down in the warm sand, their arms around each other, to watch the sunset. Karen leaned against Jerry, feeling warm and secure, and very happy. They kissed.

She couldn't believe it when she looked at her watch and it said nine o'clock. "Jerry — I've got to get back before Ann-Marie calls the police!"

He laughed and pulled her back onto the sand. "Come on — it's still early."

"No. Really. She's my guest. I'm being so rude."

"Be rude a little longer," he pleaded.

But she finally persuaded him to walk her home. At the door to her building, they threw their arms around each other and kissed, long and hard. As if we might not see each other again, Karen thought.

What a weird thought.

Karen, it's not like you to be insecure, she told herself.

As if reading her thoughts, Jerry said, "Don't worry about Renee. I'll talk to her. She and I have been through a lot together." His throat seemed to catch on these words. "She'll understand. She'll understand that it's over between her and me."

Karen kissed him again and ran inside.

She pushed open the door, prepared to apologize to Ann-Marie, to fall to her knees and beg forgiveness if necessary. But to her surprise, Ann-Marie wasn't home. A note on the refrigerator read, *I went out with some friends. Don't wait up. A.M.*

Karen stared at the note, then crumpled it up and tossed it into the wastebasket. She knew she had no right to be, but she found herself a little annoyed that Ann-Marie was never home. I'll make a point of spending tomorrow with her, she told herself.

She paced around the apartment for a while, unsure of what to do with herself, thinking about Jerry, feeling excited and happy.

He's such a great guy, she thought. Mainly, he's so *nice*. He's just so nice. Staring out the window toward the dark beach, she decided that nice was nice.

She sat down in the living room and read for a bit, trying to calm down. Then she listened to a few CDs, lying on the shaggy, white rug on the floor, staring up at the cathedral ceiling.

Finally, she felt tired enough to go to sleep. Yawning, she wrote Ann-Marie a note, saying, *Tomorrow is our day together*, and put it up on the refrigerator.

How did people ever communicate before refrigerator magnets? she wondered.

She got undressed, tossing her clothes on the armchair beside the bed, and pulled on a short nightgown. It was warm in the room, even with the window open, so she decided she didn't need the nightgown after all.

Tossing it onto the pile of clothes, she stretched, her bones cracking. She had gone from being so peppy that she couldn't sit still straight to being totally exhausted.

She turned out the lamp on the bedtable and slid into bed.

Whatever it was in bed with her was cold, and very wet, and very slimy.

Karen screamed.

And struggled to get out.

But the wet slime stuck to her arms and back and the back of her neck.

She screamed again.

And lurched out of bed, banging her knee on the bedtable.

So slimy. So cold. All down her back.

She nearly knocked over the lamp, struggling to turn it on.

Finally the light clicked on.

And she saw that her bed was filled with jellyfish.

When Ann-Marie walked in a few seconds later, Karen was still screaming.

Chapter 14

The two girls stayed up all night. It took a long time to scoop the disgusting jellyfish into a wastebasket, dump them into the garbage outside, and remove the bed linens.

"Just throw the sheets away!" Karen had cried, still hysterical. "Throw everything away!"

Even after clean linens had been put on, the sour, fishy smell remained in the apartment. "I can't sleep in that bed tonight," Karen said, shuddering.

In the small kitchen, Ann-Marie poured water from the kettle. She was silently making Karen a cup of hot herbal tea. "You can sleep in my bed," she said quietly, dunking her tea bag. "I'll take the couch."

"No, I won't be able to sleep anywhere," Karen replied angrily. "Who would *do* such a thing? It's . . . just so *disgusting*!"

"It had to be Renee, I guess," Ann-Marie said. "Do you take sugar?"

"What are you doing?" Karen asked.

"Making you a cup of tea."

"Tea? What for? I'm not sick!"

"I just thought — "

"Well, forget it." Karen paced to the window and back.

"I know you're upset, but you don't have to take it out on me," Ann-Marie protested, taking a sip of tea. She put the cup down quickly, having burned her tongue.

"How did Renee get in here?" Karen demanded. "The apartment was locked, right?"

"The window was open," Ann-Marie said, pointing to it. "She could've climbed in. You know, I saw her today."

"What?"

"In fact, I had kind of a fight with her. I wasn't going to tell you because I didn't want to upset you."

"Go ahead," Karen said, "tell me. I couldn't be any more upset."

"Well, I ran into her on Main Street, right after lunch. She immediately launched into this attack on you, about how you were trying to steal Jerry from her."

"That's what she said?"

"Yeah," Ann-Marie said. "She said a lot of crazy things. She said you were looking for trouble and didn't have any idea just how much trouble."

"She was making threats?" Karen felt sick.

"Yeah. I'd call them threats," Ann-Marie said, rolling her eyes. "It was unbelievable. She was screaming at me. I couldn't get her to shut up. I mean, people were looking at us."

"So what did you do?"

"Finally I just said, 'Renee, I'm Ann-Marie — not Karen.' And I walked away."

"How awful."

"Yes, it was. I was really upset. I mean, Renee was really losing it."

"But she had no right to scream at you because of me. I'm going over there right now," Karen decided. "I'm going to have it out with her once and for all."

"Karen, sit down. It's nearly three in the morning." Ann-Marie walked over, took Karen by the shoulders, and guided her back to the couch. "You've got to try to calm down."

"Calm down?! Did you see that disgusting pile of slime in my bed? I'll never calm down! Never!"

"Karen — this isn't like you — "

"What is she going to do to me next? That girl is sick, Ann-Marie. She's really sick. Where does she live?"

"She's staying with a friend in Santa Monica, remember? She told us the address that first night at RayJay's."

"Oh, yeah. I remember." Karen jumped up and headed to her bedroom. "Ugh. The smell. Are you sure all the windows are open? I'm going to have nightmares about jellyfish for the rest of the summer!"

"Listen, chill out, okay? Wait till morning. Then we'll go over to Renee's together if you like."

"Well . . . maybe you're right," Karen agreed. She walked over to the counter and picked up the cup of tea. She took a sip and made a face. "Needs sugar. You want a cup?"

"Yeah, I guess," Ann-Marie sighed.

They stayed up talking for another hour. Then Ann-Marie went to bed, and Karen tried to get to sleep on the living room couch. Staring up at the shifting lights and shadows on the ceiling, she saw the pink-and-purple jellyfish again, saw them glistening so wetly on her sheet, felt the cold stickiness on the back of her neck — and sat up with a jolt, about to scream again.

Get a grip on yourself, Karen, she scolded herself. This is exactly the way Renee wants you to react.

She lay back down, struggling to get comfortable, but it was hopeless. When the sky started to lighten, Karen was still wide awake. She went to the window, settled herself on the sill, and watched the sun come up.

At eight she went into her room, pulled on a pair of straight-legged jeans and a maroon sweatshirt, gave her hair a few careless swipes with a brush, and silently sneaked out of the apartment.

I don't need Ann-Marie to come with me, she thought. I've given her enough grief already. This is supposed to be her vacation, after all.

It's supposed to be mine, too, she thought, suddenly feeling very sorry for herself.

She had a sudden impulse to call Jerry, to tell him what Renee had been doing to her — the whispered phone calls, the spray-painted warning on the wall, and now the disgusting pile of jellyfish. And of course it was obvious that Renee had tried to drown her on Wednesday in the ocean. She wanted to tell Jerry everything, to let him know what Renee was really like.

But no. This was between Renee and her.

Jerry had promised that he would tell Renee it was all over between them, that he was interested in Karen now. But Karen knew she could no longer leave it to Jerry.

Renee had gone too far. Karen couldn't sit around and let herself be victimized any longer.

The morning air was chilly and wet as she hopped down the steps, searching her jeans pocket for her car keys. She let the car warm up for a few minutes. To her surprise, she didn't feel the least bit tired despite not having any sleep at all during the night.

Anger can give you real energy, she thought.

If that were true, she figured she had enough energy to keep going for *days*!

Looking in the rearview mirror at the still-deserted street, she put the car in drive, and headed toward Santa Monica. Where is everybody? she wondered, then remembered that it was Sunday morning. Who in her right mind would be out on the street at eight on a Sunday morning?

Only us angry lunatics.

There was no traffic at all, so the drive was short. The house, Karen remembered, was off Ocean Park Boulevard. Renee had spent some time describing it in detail that night, mainly because she had never stayed in a house that was painted pink with powder-blue trim.

The house shouldn't be hard to find, Karen thought, slowing down. She passed a small, triangular green park, then spotted the house between Second and Third Streets.

She pulled over to the curb, cut the engine, and stared up at the narrow, two-story house. This had to be it. It was definitely pink with blue trim.

She took a deep breath and climbed out of the car. This will all be over in a couple of minutes, she told herself.

As she walked up to the powder-blue front door, she was suddenly filled with doubts. What am I doing here? Why am I here? What am I going to say to her?

But the salt smell of the ocean in the morning air brought back the sight and feel of the jellyfish. And the reminder of the horror of the night before pushed her forward with renewed anger.

She started to knock on the door but, to her surprise, saw that it was open a few inches. She peered in through the crack. It was dark inside.

Just then the front door of the next house opened, and a balding, middle-aged man in striped pajamas stepped out onto his front stoop. He bent down to pick up the Sunday *L.A. Times* and, seeing Karen, smiled and nodded. "Nice morning," he said.

"Yeah, I guess." Karen wasn't in the mood to chat.

"They say it's going to be a hot one." Then, groaning over the weight of the enormous paper, he disappeared back into his house.

His appearance unnerved Karen somewhat. It was so unexpected. She started to knock again, then changed her mind and called into the house. "Renee — are you there?"

No reply.

Karen pushed the front door open a bit wider. The door squeaked as she pushed it. "Renee? Renee?"

Silence.

Karen stepped into the small entryway. She peeked into the dark living room. No one there. The room was furnished with chrome-and-white-leather easy chairs and an enormous, circular glass coffee table, all very expensive-looking.

"Renee? Anybody home?"

Silence.

"Renee — I want to talk to you!"

She walked quickly through a short hallway and into the kitchen in the back. This room was brighter since the sun was pouring in through the window.

Karen's eyes lit on the sink, piled high with dirty, white china dishes and bowls. Then she saw a half-eaten sandwich on a plate and an open bottle of Coke on the Formica and butcher-block island in the middle of the room.

Then her eyes wandered down to the floor, and she saw two bare feet, the toes pointing up.

Her breath caught in her throat.

She walked closer.

"Renee?"

She peered around the island and saw a girl lying on her back, her mouth open in a frozen O of horror, her eyes wide, unmoving, staring up at the ceiling.

"Renee?"

She was wearing shorty pajamas.

"Renee?"

Her frizzy hair circled her head, standing straight out at the sides. There was an enormous bump on her forehead.

Karen reached down and touched Renee's arm. It was cold. As cold as death.

Renee was dead.

Karen dropped the limp, cold arm and stood up. She took a deep breath and prayed that she wouldn't start screaming.

Chapter 15

The police station, with its lime-green cinderblock walls and glass brick separators, had a California flair to it. It was brightly lit, carpeted, and had two miniature palm trees guarding the double-doored glass entranceway, not at all the stereotypical police station of movies or TV.

As she sat on the green plastic bench, waiting her turn to be questioned, Karen would have preferred the more traditional dark, dingy station house. She wanted everything to be gray, even black. She wanted to close her eyes and disappear into darkness, disappear from this nightmare.

How could this be happening?

She had called the L.A.P.D. immediately, pushing 911, with fingers that wouldn't stop trembling. She had told the officers who arrived a few minutes later everything — who the girl lying on the floor was, how she had happened to find her, how she happened to know her. The friend Renee had been staying with wasn't there. She was out of the country for the whole summer, and the police had ruled Renee's friend out.

There really wasn't much more Karen could tell. She had no idea who murdered Renee.

They had already questioned Jerry for more than an hour. Now Ann-Marie was in there being grilled. Karen was next. But why? What more could she tell them?

What good would more questions do? All the questions in the world couldn't bring back Renee. All of the questions in the world couldn't remove the picture of Renee's body in the kitchen from Karen's mind, a picture she knew she would be seeing again and again for the rest of her life.

She had been sitting there on the bench, staring at the unlikely palm trees for about twenty minutes, when her mother arrived, frantic as usual, with her lawyer Ross Garland. "Karen — what on earth? This is so horrible," her mother said, dropping down onto the bench beside her. "Are you all right?"

"I guess," Karen said. What could she say? That she saw Renee's pale, white body every time she closed her eyes?

Mr. Garland started to say something, but the door opened, and Ann-Marie came hurrying out, looking as flushed as her pink T-shirt, and very frightened.

"They think I did it! I know they do!" she exclaimed to Karen, ignoring everyone else.

"Ann-Marie — what do you mean? How can they?" Karen's mother demanded.

"Oh. Hi, Mrs. Mandell," Ann-Marie said, barely

looking at her. "Some friend of Renee's saw me fighting on Main Street with Renee yesterday afternoon. When they heard about what happened to Renee on the radio, they phoned the police. I tried to explain to them that I had no reason to kill Renee. I hardly knew her! But they think I did it! I know they do!"

"Calm down," Mr. Garland said, putting a hand gently on Ann-Marie's shoulder. "The police are a little more sophisticated than that."

"Thank you," said a deep voice. Everyone looked up to see a grim-faced police detective. He was young-looking with blond hair and narrow blue eyes set close together. He was wearing dark brown, pleated slacks and a short-sleeved, white shirt with a dark blue necktie pulled down a few inches over an unbuttoned collar.

"I'm Detective Franklin," he said, looking at Karen's mother. He turned to Ann-Marie. "We don't think you did it," he told her. "We're questioning everyone we can. But you're not a suspect."

Ann-Marie didn't seem to believe him. "That's what the police always say before they spring a trap."

"This isn't TV," he said brusquely. "Sometimes I wish it were."

A tall, uniformed lieutenant came walking by. "Have you reached the girl's parents?" Detective Franklin asked.

"Not yet. They're in Europe, somewhere outside Paris. We're still working on it. The victim's cousin is coming up from Anaheim."

Franklin nodded. He looked down at Karen. "You're next."

"This is my mother and our attorney, Mr. Garland," Karen said, climbing to her feet, surprised by how shaky her legs felt.

"Why don't you wait out here and have a cup of coffee?" Franklin told Mrs. Mandell. "The machine has surprisingly good coffee." He motioned for Karen and the attorney to follow him.

His office was small but cheerful. He had a large, psychedelic-style Grateful Dead poster behind his desk and several thriving, hanging vines over his window. He didn't wait for Karen and Garland to sit down before he began firing questions at Karen.

"How long did you know Renee Watson? When did you meet? Why were you at her house this morning? If you just met her last Monday, how did you know where she lived? Had you been there before? How well do you know her boyfriend?"

Karen answered the questions as best as she could, staring hard at the orange-and-green poster behind the detective. As she replied, several of her own questions ran through her mind: Should I tell him about the jellyfish? Should I tell him how I almost drowned because of her? Should I tell him how I feel about Jerry, how Jerry planned to break up with her because of me?

She decided no. What good would it do to tell the police detective about any of that? It would only make it look as if Karen had a real motive for killing Renee. It would only make Karen a serious suspect in the murder. And since Karen knew she wasn't the murderer, she decided it would serve no useful purpose to reveal those things.

"How well do you know Jerry Gaines?"

"Not very well. I met him last Monday, too. I've seen him a few times since."

"On dates?"

"Not really. I knew he was dating Renee."

"But you were attracted to him?"

"A little."

I'm doing okay, Karen thought. This isn't so hard. It would be a lot harder if I really had something to hide.

The questioning went on for nearly twenty minutes. It became hot and stuffy in Detective Franklin's small office, but he made no move to open the window or turn on the air conditioner. He kept asking the same questions again and again, reworking them, then asking them again.

He's trying to trip me up, Karen realized. He's looking for an inconsistency. He's really pretty clever.

When he finally led her back to the front waiting room, she felt exhausted. Ann-Marie and her mother were seated side by side on the green bench, talking quietly.

"I've got to get home. I'm missing my son's birthday party," Garland said, looking anxiously at his watch.

"It was so nice of you to hurry over on a Sunday," Mrs. Mandell said, getting up and taking Garland's hand.

"Don't worry," Garland told Karen, starting toward the double doors. "Try to forget about it. I know that's not easy. But try." And he disappeared out the door.

Before the door could close, two uniformed officers pushed through it. They were grappling with a young man, who was obviously displeased about having to accompany them. "Let go of me!" Karen heard the young man growl, and she recognized the voice before she saw the face.

It was Vince.

"You've got no right," he was shouting. "Why are you bringing me here?" One of the officers gave Vince a hard shove toward Detective Franklin's office. Vince nearly stumbled, but the other policeman caught him by the arm.

"I didn't do anything," Vince protested.

"Then you won't mind answering a few questions," the first policeman said.

For a brief second, Vince turned and his eyes caught Karen's. He didn't seem to recognize her. Maybe he was pretending not to. Maybe he was concentrating so hard on his struggles with the policemen, he didn't see her.

Karen felt a chill run through her body. Vince disappeared into Detective Franklin's office. The door was slammed behind him.

Did Vince kill Renee?

She didn't realize that her mother was tugging on her sleeve. "This is a little too much real life for me," Mrs. Mandell said. "Come home with me now?"

"Hey, do I look *that* bad?" Karen asked, still thinking about Vince.

"You don't look good," Mrs. Mandell said in her usual, maddeningly direct way.

"I . . . uh . . . didn't sleep well last night," Karen told her. She looked at Ann-Marie, who still looked pale and shaken. "But I think we'll go back to Daddy's," Karen said. "He's expecting us."

"Where is your father, anyhow?" Mrs. Mandell asked, suddenly remembering her former husband's existence. "Why isn't he here?"

"I called you instead," Karen said, thinking quickly. "You know how Daddy is in an emergency."

Mrs. Mandell seemed to find that a reasonable excuse for his absence. Karen secretly breathed a sigh of relief. "Ann-Marie and I are going to try to enjoy the rest of our month together," she told her mother.

Mrs. Mandell looked at her doubtfully. "If only you didn't look so terrible. I really wish you'd come home with me. Both of you."

For a brief second, Karen considered it. It would be nice to be safe and cozy back home with her mother to take care of them. But no. She wanted to see Jerry. She *had* to see Jerry, to see how he was taking this, to make sure he was okay. He must be terribly, terribly upset. After all, he and Renee had been going together for years.

She wondered if Jerry had any idea who might have killed her.

She wondered what he had told the police.

"No, thanks, Mom," she said, and draped her arms around her mother in a long hug. "Ann-Marie and I will go back to Venice. But I'll call you tonight. Promise."

The three of them walked quickly out of the police station. The fresh afternoon air felt good on Karen's face. She took a deep breath and stretched. Having no sleep the night before was beginning to catch up with her.

They said good-bye to Mrs. Mandell, who, still looking very worried, headed to her car. Karen had parked the Mustang a few blocks in the other direction.

She and Ann-Marie were only half a block from the police station, walking slowly, silently, just glad to be outdoors, when a tall, red-haired girl in white denim jeans and an orange top that clashed with her hair, stepped in front of them on the sidewalk.

"Are you Karen?" she asked, looking at Karen with a nervous expression on her face, her large, dark eyes darting back and forth between Karen and Ann-Marie.

"Yes," Karen answered uncertainly. "How did you know my name?"

"It doesn't matter," the girl said mysteriously. "I just want to warn you to stay away from Jerry."

"What?" Ann-Marie cried, appearing more startled than Karen.

"Who *are* you?" Karen asked angrily. "Are *you* his girlfriend, too?!"

"I don't want to make a scene," the girl said, ignoring Karen's questions. "Just — please — " and her dark eyes brimmed with tears as she started to plead — "please stay away from Jerry. I'm . . . warning you."

She turned and hurried away, taking long, quick strides across the sidewalk.

But Karen ran after her, caught up, and stepped in front of her. "Who are you? Answer me. Why are you warning me? Who are you?"

The girl shook her head, her red hair quivering about her face. Finally, she said, "I'm Jerry's sister." She ducked past Karen and started to run.

"Well, Jerry's old enough to make his own decisions!" Karen shouted after her. She started to chase her, but Ann-Marie held her back.

"Come on. We've got to get home. Enough," Ann-Marie said softly.

Karen was still breathing hard, her eyes following the girl until she disappeared around the corner. "Why would Jerry's sister be waiting here for me? It doesn't make any sense."

"Nothing makes any sense," Ann-Marie said. "Nothing at all. Do you think she's the one who's been trying to frighten you away from Jerry? Not Renee?"

An even more frightening thought crossed Karen's mind.

"Do you think Jerry's sister killed Renee?"

"Huh?"

Karen hadn't realized she was talking out loud. "Just a thought."

They drove back, both of them chattering without stop about what had happened. It was almost as if they were afraid to be silent, afraid that silence would give them time to think, that if they could keep talking, keep tuned in to each other, they could shut the real horror out.

But Karen knew she couldn't shut it out for long. Every time she closed her eyes, she saw Renee again. Every few seconds, she was back in that kitchen, looking down at the bump on Renee's head, making the horrifying discovery all over again.

"I've never known anyone who died," Ann-Marie said, as Karen parked the Mustang across from the apartment house.

Karen climbed out of the car wearily. The sun was lowering itself behind the houses and apartment buildings on Speedway. The sky was red. All of the buildings looked red, as red as blood.

"I guess we should get some dinner," she said.

"I — I'm not very hungry," Ann-Marie told her, evening shadows darkening her face.

"Hi," a voice called. Jerry stepped away from the apartment house wall and walked toward them slowly, his hands in his jeans pockets.

It took Karen a moment to recognize him. His usually neat hair was windblown and standing on end. As he came close, Karen saw that his eyes were red-rimmed, his cheeks were puffy, as if he had been crying.

"Are you okay?" Karen asked.

He took her hand and squeezed it. His hand was ice-cold.

"Yeah, I'm okay, I guess."

He stood there, leaning toward her, staring at her, still holding her hand.

"I — I'm sorry," Karen stammered.

"I'm sorry you had to be the one to find her," Jerry said, his voice quavering. He let go of her hand and looked away.

"It's really terrible," Ann-Marie said awkwardly.

"I just can't believe it," Jerry said, still looking across the street. "I just talked to her last night, and today — "

"The police will find whoever did it," Ann-Marie said.

Jerry didn't respond for a long while. "What difference does it make?" He turned to Karen. "I just feel so guilty. I was going over there tonight to break up with her. And now — "

Karen raised a finger to his lips. "Shhh. You shouldn't feel guilty. You didn't do anything to feel guilty about." And then she added, "Oh. By the way, your sister stopped us when we came out of the police station."

"Huh?" Jerry's eyes narrowed in surprise.

"Your sister — she stopped me. She — "

He put a hand on her shoulder. "Karen — what are you talking about? I don't have a sister."

Chapter 16

"Do you think Vince killed her?" Karen asked.

She, Ann-Marie, and Jerry were sitting in the back booth at RayJay's. They had the entire row of booths to themselves, the restaurant uncrowded this early on a Sunday night. They had ordered a pizza, but none of them had much of an appetite.

Once or twice Karen had attempted to change the subject of discussion away from Renee. But they quickly realized it was pointless trying to talk about anything else. And again, talking about it, Karen realized, helped them to keep calm, to keep from falling apart and giving in to a strong feeling of terror that lurked just beyond their words.

"I don't know," Jerry said, tapping his long fingers on the Formica tabletop.

"Did Vince know Renee?" Ann-Marie asked, taking a small bite from her slice, then dropping it back on the plate.

"I think he followed her once on the boardwalk," Jerry said. "You know, whistled at her or something. But I don't think he really knew her."

"So he'd have no reason to kill her," Karen said, thinking about her motorcycle ride to Santa Monica with Vince.

Could she have been riding with a killer?

Could she be so attracted to a killer?

"He's a dangerous character," Jerry said, staring down at his pizza slice. "He could have done it — just for a thrill."

"No. He wouldn't do that," Karen said. The words just slipped out of her mouth before she had a chance to think about them.

"Well, the police thought he could have," Jerry replied, angry for some reason.

Karen was startled by the heatedness of his reply. "Sorry. I didn't mean — "

His expression immediately softened. He took her hand over the table. "No. I'm sorry. I don't know *what* I'm saying. I don't know anything. At first, I was so stupid — you know what I thought?"

"What?" Karen asked.

"I thought Renee committed suicide because of me. Because she knew I was going to break up with her. Do you know how awful I felt?" His voice cracked. His face reddened. He closed his eyes. "Pretty stupid, huh?"

"Jerry, please — "

"Well, the police must've thought I was pretty stupid," he continued, nervously picking at his slice of pizza. "When I sat down in that detective's office, I asked if Renee left a note. Can you imagine? Someone clubbed her to death, and I was asking if she left a suicide note!"

He laughed, a mirthless, painful laugh.

"Jerry, stop." Karen removed her hand from under his. "There's no point in torturing yourself. It won't do you any good to make yourself feel guilty over this."

"I guess you're right," he sighed. He leaned back against the red vinyl seat and closed his eyes.

"You've been awfully quiet," Karen said to Ann-Marie.

"I just can't believe I'm a murder suspect," Ann-Marie said softly, tugging at a short tangle of blonde hair. "I — I'd like to go home."

"Back to New York?"

"Yeah. But the detective said I can't leave town. Do you believe it?" She shredded her paper napkin between her hands and let the pieces flutter to the table.

"I'm sorry," Karen told her friend. "Now *I* feel guilty. You're a prisoner here. It was supposed to be a fun vacation, and — "

She stopped because something at the restaurant window caught her eye.

A boy. With straight brown hair.

He was staring at them from outside on the sidewalk, nose pressed against the window glass, shielding his eyes with both hands.

It took Karen a few seconds to recognize him. But she was sure she was right.

Mike!

Why was Mike watching them like that? What was he doing here?

Without saying a word to Ann-Marie or Jerry,

she climbed out of the booth and hurried up the aisle to the front door.

When he saw her coming, Mike's face filled with surprise, and he took off.

By the time Karen got to the sidewalk, he had disappeared.

Chapter 17

"I'm going for a walk. Want to come?"

Ann-Marie climbed to her feet and adjusted her bathing suit.

Karen sat up and looked around. The ocean was calm, the blue-green waves low and nearly as flat as a lake. Above them, two sea gulls swooped and climbed, wings outspread, a billowy white cloud for their background.

It was the next afternoon, and both girls had thought that a few hours of baking in the sun might help them relax. But Ann-Marie couldn't sit still.

"Well, are you coming?" Ann-Marie asked impatiently.

"No. Think I'll stay here." Karen settled back down on the beach blanket and closed her eyes. "Wake me up when you get back, okay?"

"Have you got suntan stuff on?" Ann-Marie asked, slipping a light cotton shirt over her bikini top. "The sun is pretty strong today."

"I don't need it. I want to burn for a while. Have a nice walk."

"Okay. Have a nice roast." Ann-Marie headed off in the direction of the Venice Pavilion, walking close to the shore, the water lapping over her feet.

Karen looked up at the sky through her sunglasses. The sea gulls and the cloud had disappeared. The sun was beginning to feel like a real summer sun.

She closed her eyes and saw Renee lying dead on the floor in the kitchen. Then she saw Vince being dragged into the police station. Then she saw Mike staring into the window at RayJay's.

If only I could close my eyes and just see *nothing*, she thought.

She had been up nearly the whole night. Renee had kept her up — poor, dead Renee.

Renee. Renee. Renee.

Renee probably would enjoy the fact that she was haunting Karen now.

What a wicked thing to think, Karen scolded herself.

Poor Renee.

She drifted into a light, troubled sleep. She was awakened a short time later by a hand on her shoulder. Sitting up with a start, she realized that her arm had fallen asleep.

"Hey."

She looked up, startled to see Vince staring down at her, smiling, the dimples deep in his cheeks. He was wearing faded cutoffs and no shirt. His chest was broad and hairless and tanned.

"Vince."

"Sorry. Did I scare you?"

Something about the smile on his face frightened her. He seemed secretly delighted that he had scared her.

"Vince, I didn't expect — "

"How you doing?" His smile faded. "You okay? I mean — "

"Yeah. I guess. I didn't sleep last night. Every time I close my eyes — "

"Come take a walk with me, okay?" he interrupted, reaching his hands down for her. He took her hands and started to pull her up.

He was stronger than Karen realized. He pulled her to her feet so easily, she felt frightened again.

He's strong enough to kill someone, she thought.

She shook her arm, trying to make it stop tingling.

"Come on. Just a short walk," he said, staring into her eyes. "Or will your *boyfriend* mind?" He sneered as he said the word boyfriend, making it sound like a term of pure disgust.

"Okay," she said hesitantly. "You don't have to pull my arms off."

He looked genuinely embarrassed. "Sorry." He turned and started walking down to the water, expecting her to follow.

She held back for a few seconds. What does he want? she asked herself. What if he really did kill Renee?

He couldn't have, she decided. His toughness, it's mostly an act. I can tell.

She jogged across the sand to catch up with him. "Ouch. The sand is really hot!" she cried, slipping and catching his arm to hold herself up.

"It'll be cooler down by the water," he said, staring out at the gently rippling ocean. A sailboat far out on the horizon seemed to be standing still, its sail a small white triangle against the blue sky.

She held onto him, the water splashing over their feet and legs as they walked. His arm felt solid, hard. He's like a rock, she thought.

I need a rock now. Someone solid. Someone to lean on.

Stop being stupid, Karen, she thought, shaking her head.

The cold spray felt good on her face. She closed her eyes and saw Renee.

"The police let you go?" she asked. A stupid question.

"Yeah, sure." He frowned and kicked at a shell with his bare foot, missing.

"I saw you there."

"I know."

He started walking a little faster. The beach curved to the right, past the line of brown rocks where she had nearly drowned. She looked back at the beach. It was nearly deserted here.

Where is he taking me? she thought, chilled more by her thoughts than by the cold spray off the ocean.

Maybe I don't want to walk too far with him.

"Did they ask you a lot of questions?" she asked, looking back at the lifeguard tower, which was now far in the distance.

"Yeah. A waste of time. My time and theirs."

"Well, why'd they bring you there?" she asked,

feeling stupid again. What she really wanted to ask was: Did you kill Renee?

"Whenever something bad happens, they find an excuse to bring me in. My pals, too."

"They do?"

"Yeah. They do. But the whole thing was a crock. I mean, I didn't even know the girl. And I wasn't anywhere near Santa Monica. I was right here in Venice. My buddies backed me up."

He stopped at a large piece of driftwood, a long log burned black and made smooth by the sea. He grinned at her, but it wasn't his usual relaxed grin. He looked nervous. "I don't look like a killer — do I?"

Karen laughed, a phony laugh. "Of course not." She wondered if she looked as nervous as he did. She could feel the fear begin to tighten her throat. Looking around, she realized they were the only ones in view.

Where was everybody? Why had he brought her here?

"That poor girl," she said, picturing Renee again. "She and your boyfriend were . . . uh. . . ."

"He's not my boyfriend," Karen said, flustered. She knew she sounded like a ten-year-old. Why did Vince always make her feel so weird?

She was afraid of him. And she was attracted to him at the same time. He was just so different from anyone she'd ever known.

"Maybe we should start back," she said, trying not to reveal that she was frightened, but her voice sounded tight and high-pitched.

"Hey, look at that!" he cried, pointing to a splash of water out several dozen yards in the ocean. "Look — there it goes again."

She followed his gaze and saw a long silver fish leap out of the water.

"How pretty."

Without warning, he pulled her to him and wrapped his arms around her, pressing her against his warm, bare chest. He leaned his head down and kissed her.

Uttering a low, startled cry, she began to pull back. But she was overcome by a rush of feeling.

He was so warm. His chest felt so hard, so rock-solid hard.

He kissed her hungrily. He needed her.

And she needed him.

She kissed him back.

When the kiss was finished, she pushed herself away from him, her hands on his chest. He let her go, dropping his arms to his sides.

"Vince, what are we doing?"

He grinned, the deep dimples making him look so . . . devilish.

Karen felt terribly confused.

She thought about Jerry, so good-looking, so sensitive, and caring . . . so *nice*.

She stared at Vince, his short, spiky hair, the diamond stud in his ear, the bold, black tattoo on his hand.

How could she like two boys who were so totally different?

Vince moved toward her, about to pull her into

his arms again. But Karen raised her hands as if to shield herself from him. "No. I don't think so."

He stopped. He looked surprised.

"I'm feeling a little mixed up," she said, embarrassed.

"You have great eyes," he said.

"I think I just want to go back to my blanket now."

He started to protest, but quickly relented. "Okay." He started to lead the way.

"No." She didn't follow. "By myself. I'd just like to walk by myself for a while, try to figure things out. Or something."

He shrugged. "Tough times, huh?"

She couldn't decide if he was sincere or if he was making fun of her. "Listen, I'll see you, okay?"

"Yeah. Okay." He stood and watched her hurry off.

She started jogging across the sand, her heart pounding. She turned back once and saw that he hadn't moved from the spot near the driftwood. He waved, and she waved back and kept jogging.

It felt good to run, the warm sand so soft under her bare feet, the sun on her face, the air so warm and fresh. If only she could run and run and run — and not stop to think.

She saw her blanket up on the beach. Ann-Marie wasn't back yet. Karen decided to keep going. She jogged for another twenty minutes or so, until she was breathing hard, bathed in perspiration, her legs aching.

Where was Ann-Marie? Karen hoped she would

run into her heading back. Maybe she had gone up to the boardwalk.

Karen took several deep breaths and began walking back to the blanket. The slower speed allowed her thoughts to catch up with her. She relived the kiss with Vince. And that made her think of Friday night in Malibu, kissing Jerry in the shadow of that abandoned beach house.

With Renee looking on.

Was that only three nights before?

It seemed like a lifetime.

It *was* a lifetime, for Renee.

She dropped down on a beach blanket. Where was Ann-Marie? Karen looked up and down the beach but didn't see her.

She reached into her bag and pulled out the plastic bottle of suntan lotion. A folded-up slip of white paper fell onto the blanket. Curious, she put down the suntan lotion and picked up the paper, unfolding it quickly.

The typewritten words jumped out at her and then burned themselves into her eyes.

The same message was typed over and over again, in all capital letters, without any punctuation.

STAY AWAY FROM JERRY STAY AWAY FROM JERRY STAY AWAY FROM JERRY STAY AWAY FROM JERRY

Disgusted, Karen crumpled up the sheet of paper and tossed it down on the beach blanket.

Who could have put that in her beach bag?

She picked up the bottle of suntan lotion,

squeezed a white blob of it onto her shoulder, and started to massage it in.

The sudden stab of pain was so sharp, so overwhelming that at first she didn't recognize it as pain.

Her shoulder — her hand — they were burning, burning.

I'm on fire, she thought.

What were those hideous shrieks she heard?

Grabbing her shoulder in agony, Karen was in so much pain, she didn't realize that it was *she* who was screaming at the top of her lungs.

Chapter 18

Dr. Martinez put a hand gently on Karen's other shoulder and led her out of the examining room. "How does it feel now?" He smiled in that reassuring way that all doctors have, a closed-mouth smile beneath his black mustache.

"It aches a little," Karen said, disappointed that the pain hadn't completely gone away.

"It will continue to ache as it heals," the doctor said, nodding at a passing nurse. Her rubber heels squeaked down the long hospital corridor. "You were very lucky."

"Lucky?" Karen rolled her eyes.

"Well, you were lucky you only spread the cream on the one shoulder. If you had rubbed it over a larger portion of your body, the burn — "

He was interrupted by a young black man in a starched, green lab coat who appeared from around the corner, a clipboard in his hands. "Lab report," he said brusquely, shoving the clipboard into Dr. Martinez's hands.

Martinez frowned in concentration as he glanced

over the top sheet. "This is the analysis of what was in your suntan lotion bottle," he told Karen, still reading.

Karen had a stab of pain in her hand. She wanted to scratch it, but it was heavily bandaged. The palm had been pretty badly burned.

"Any of your friends into chemistry?" Dr. Martinez asked, handing the clipboard back to the lab assistant, who disappeared as quickly and as silently as he had arrived.

"No, I don't think so," Karen replied, confused.

"Well, somebody managed to mix a pretty good solution of hydrochloric acid into your lotion."

"Acid?"

"Yep. Do you know of anyone who might want to play a really cruel trick on you? A deadly trick?"

Deadly? The word made Karen shudder.

Who had done it? Who was there on the beach with her? Only Ann-Marie and Vince.

"Could it have been done in the store, by some crazy person? Or at the factory?" Karen suggested hopefully.

Please, please, don't let it be someone I know. Someone I like.

"Well, that's the first thing I would've said," Dr. Martinez said, walking her slowly down the long, white-walled corridor. "But the bottle is two-thirds empty."

"You mean — "

"I mean you've used it before, right? You've been using the lotion with no problem up to now."

"Yeah, that's right," Karen said, a sinking feeling

in her stomach. "I've been using it all month."

"So someone tampered with it recently," Dr. Martinez suggested. "Someone added the hydrochloric acid very recently."

"But who would do that to me?" Karen blurted out, her bandaged shoulder starting to burn and throb.

"I can't answer that," he said. "I think we have no choice but to call the police."

"The police?"

Karen's mind flashed back to Detective Franklin's office, to the endless questions, repeated over and over. "No, please."

"If we don't inform the police, we at least have to inform your parents. You're still a minor, and — "

"But my parents are away," Karen said. It was only half a lie. "They're . . . out of the country. I'm sort of on my own until they get back."

They were interrupted by a call for Dr. Martinez on the loudspeaker. "I've got to check on that," he said, pulling back the sleeve of his white coat to glance at his watch. "Stay right here, okay? We've got to settle this. Don't move. I'll be right back." He took off in a fast walk around the corner.

As soon as he was out of sight, Karen headed to the front reception area. I'm getting out of here, she told herself. She hated hospitals, the sterile look of them, the disgusting medicinal smells, the sick people walking the halls. She didn't want her mother to know about this. Mrs. Mandell would force Karen to come home. And she would find out that Karen had lied about her dad staying with them in Venice.

No. No way. And she certainly didn't want to see that police detective with his accusing blue eyes again, either.

"Hey, Karen — wait!"

She was past the reception desk, heading to the front doors.

"Karen!"

She kept going. She just wanted to get away.

A hand grabbed her good shoulder. She spun around, expecting a confrontation with Dr. Martinez. "Vince!" she cried. "I didn't know you were still here. I didn't think you'd wait."

He looked embarrassed. "Yeah, well. I wanted to see how you were."

"I'm okay, thanks to you," she said, giving him a warm smile. If he hadn't pulled her off the beach, gotten her onto the back of his motorcycle, and bombed off to the hospital at the speed of light, her burns might have been a lot more serious.

"What was it?"

The way he asked the question made her suspicious. Had he done it? Switched bottles, maybe?

No. Of course not. Don't get totally paranoid, she scolded herself. You can't start suspecting every single person you know. This boy came to your rescue. He wouldn't have done that if he had been the one trying to hurt you — would he?

She thought about the typewritten note with its repeated warning. What had she done with that note? Left it on the sand, probably.

Someone was getting serious about keeping her from Jerry. Was it the same person who had murdered Renee?

"Well?"

"Oh. Sorry." Karen was so lost in her own thoughts, she'd forgotten that Vince had asked her a question. "I don't know. Something wrong with the suntan lotion," she said. She tried to shrug but it sent a stab of pain down from her shoulder. "They're still testing it."

"What did the doctor say?" Vince asked.

"Just that it'll heal. I have to change the bandages every day. Keep it wrapped up. Keep it out of the sun. There goes my perfect tan. I guess you won't be interested in me anymore," she joked, giving him a sly smile.

"Who's interested?" He smiled back, revealing his dimples.

How can I be interested in him? Karen thought. He's not my type at all. My mom would have a fit if she knew I was hanging out with a *gang leader*. Vince's tattoo would probably give her the cold shakes for a month!

"I can go swimming in a few days, if I wear a wet suit," she said. "So I guess it's not too bad."

"Want a lift home?"

She suddenly felt extremely weary. The adrenalin rush from all the pain, all the terror was wearing off. "Yeah. That would be nice."

He drove almost carefully on the way to her apartment, only running a few lights and riding on the wrong side of the road for only a few blocks.

She guessed he was being careful because of her hand and shoulder.

She leaned forward as he drove the motorcycle through the late afternoon traffic, holding onto him with her one good hand, pressing her face against the back of his leather jacket.

He's someone to lean on, she thought. He's so solid. And he smells so good. She closed her eyes, hoping it might make the trip go faster. Or last forever. At this point, she didn't care which.

With her eyes closed, she pictured Renee, dead on the kitchen floor.

Poor, dead Renee.

Go away, Renee. Please — go away.

And then she pictured Ann-Marie.

Ann-Marie, where were you when I was burned? Ann-Marie.

Karen opened her eyes, but Ann-Marie's face stayed in her mind. A cold feeling spread over her body, and she knew it wasn't just from the rush of wind on her as they sped through the narrow Venice streets.

Ann-Marie had said she was going for a walk, but then never returned. Ann-Marie had shared the blanket with her. Never mind that. Ann-Marie had shared the apartment with her. Ann-Marie could have tampered with the suntan lotion at any time.

As Karen approached the apartment, the case against Ann-Marie grew in her mind. Where had Ann-Marie been spending her time, anyway? Karen had seen so little of her since she'd arrived. When Karen got the threatening call, Ann-Marie had been out. And then . . . and then . . . the can of spray paint in Ann-Marie's dresser drawer. The jellyfish in the bed. It would be easier for Ann-Marie to put them there than anyone else. She had a key to the apartment, after all.

Suddenly Karen was remembering back, back before Ann-Marie moved east. She was remembering the jealous rages, always over one boy or another. Ann-Marie had always been jealous of Karen.

But was she jealous enough now to hurt Karen? Was she so desperate to have Jerry for herself?

It didn't make any sense.

Did it?

Vince screeched the motorcycle to a halt, almost sending Karen flying over the handlebars. "Whoa," he said, climbing off quickly. "Sorry."

Karen climbed off, her shoulder aching, and looked up at the apartment house. Home at last.

But who was that running out the front door?

It was Mike.

Mike?

Yes. Without a doubt. It was Mike.

Mike saw her, then immediately turned his face away, leaped over the low hedge, and took off, running at top speed.

That's odd, Karen thought. What on earth was Mike doing here? And why was he leaving in such a hurry?

Confused, she turned back to Vince, who was standing awkwardly with his large hands stuffed in his jeans pockets. "Thanks, Vince. For everything."

"Should I come in?"

"No. I'll be okay." She started up the concrete stairs. "Thanks again. You were great."

She turned back at the entranceway to the building. He was still standing there by his motorcycle, watching her, the golden afternoon sun on his face.

She gave him a weary wave and walked inside. The spray-painted wall hadn't been cleaned, even though the landlord had promised to take care of it. She sighed loudly as she passed it.

I just want to get into bed, she thought.

She turned the key, pushed open the door, and stepped into the living room.

What was that behind the armchair?

It was a pair of feet.

Ann-Marie's feet.

Lying on the floor.

"Ann-Marie?"

Why was she lying facedown on the floor?

Chapter 19

Karen's breath caught in her throat. She could feel the blood rushing to her head. Dizzy, she grabbed onto the side of the doorway.

No, no, no, she thought. And the picture of Renee haunted her once again.

"Ann-Marie?"

Ann-Marie stood up quickly. "Oh. Hi."

"Oh, thank goodness!"

"Karen — what's the matter?" Ann-Marie's face filled with concern. Leaning on the chairback, she pulled herself to her feet. "Your shoulder — what happened?"

"Ann-Marie — you just gave me such a scare."

"Huh?"

"I saw you lying on the floor and I thought — "

"Oh! Oh, no. I'm sorry, Karen. I was just — my pendant — the chain broke. It fell behind the chair, and I was picking it up. I didn't hear you come in. I was just — "

Why did she look so embarrassed? Her normally pale skin was nearly scarlet.

"Your shoulder — what's with the bandage? Look at your hand. What did you do to yourself?"

"I got burned," Karen said, her suspicions about her friend coming back to her now that she realized Ann-Marie was okay.

"Sunburned?"

"No. Burned. Where were you, anyway, Ann-Marie?"

"I went for a walk. A long walk. I met some people, and then when I got back, you were gone." She walked over to Karen and took Karen's bag for her. "I never dreamed you were hurt or anything. Where did you go? Come. Sit down. Tell me what happened. Want a Coke or anything?"

Ann-Marie walked into the attached kitchen and pulled open the refrigerator door, burying her head inside it. Like an ostrich trying to escape, Karen thought.

"Ann-Marie, come back. We have to talk. I just saw Mike outside."

"Huh?" She slammed the refrigerator door shut and spun around.

"I saw Mike. Was he here?"

"Okay, okay," Ann-Marie said quietly, coming back into the room and dropping down on the chair across from Karen. Her green eyes burned into Karen's. "You had to find out sooner or later, I suppose."

Karen was totally confused now. "Find out about . . . ?"

"About Mike and me," Ann-Marie said, sighing. "We've been seeing each other."

"You and Mike!?" Karen's voice slid up to where only dogs could hear it.

"I was worried you wouldn't approve. I didn't know if you were still interested in him or not. I felt so guilty sneaking around with him. But I just didn't want to confront you about it. I guess I should've said something right away. I just — "

"You mean that's where you've been all the time? With Mike?"

Ann-Marie nodded her head guiltily, her face still flushed.

Karen felt like laughing out loud. And so she did.

Ann-Marie's mouth dropped open in bewilderment. "What's so funny?"

Karen wanted to tell her, but she was laughing too hard.

Here she was, suspecting her friend of the most hideous things, wondering why Ann-Marie always looked so uncomfortable, so *guilty* — and all she was doing was seeing Mike!

Karen laughed until tears rolled down her cheeks. Finally, gasping for breath, she forced herself to stop.

"Does this mean you don't care if I see Mike?" Ann-Marie asked, which started Karen laughing all over again.

"Stop me. Please. I'm hysterical!" Karen exclaimed, ignoring the pain in her shoulder and lying down on the white shag rug and staring up at the ceiling, tears of laughter running down the sides of her face. "I'm hysterical!"

"I don't get it," Ann-Marie said. She started

laughing, too. "What are we laughing about?"

"I don't know. But it's better than what's been going on here up till now," Karen said.

The phone rang, immediately jarring them out of their laughter. Karen sat up, wiping her cheeks with her hands. The phone continued to ring. She stared at it, considering not picking it up.

But what if it's Daddy? she thought.

Or Jerry.

Or Vince.

Jerry or Vince?

She climbed to her feet, walked over to the table, and picked up the receiver. "Hello?"

"Hello, is this Karen?"

"Yes, it is," she said warily, trying to remember where she had heard the girl's voice before. "Who's this?"

"This is Jerry's sister. I — "

"I don't know who you *really* are," Karen angrily interrupted, "but I know you're not Jerry's sister."

The girl at the other end started to say something, but Karen slammed down the receiver.

When was the horror going to stop? she wondered, feeling her arm throb. When were the threats going to stop?

She slumped back to the floor and closed her eyes. She no longer felt like laughing.

Her shoulder hurt.

Someone had tried to kill her, she realized.

Someone had tried to burn her to death.

No, she didn't feel like laughing. Now she just felt very tired. And very scared.

Chapter 20

"Are you sure you should be going in the water?"

Karen pulled the hood of her new wet suit over her hair and made a face at Jerry. "Yes, I'm sure it's okay, Mom."

He reached over and tenderly helped her tuck a strand of hair under the hood. "Don't make fun of me," he said seriously. "I'm just concerned about you, you know."

She picked up the snorkeling mask and straightened the straps. "Well, I wouldn't have come to this beach party if I couldn't go in the water, would I?"

She looked back at the other kids, who were sunbathing, standing around talking in small groups, playing volleyball, or preparing to go swimming or snorkeling. There was nearly a hundred of them here at the cove on this Friday afternoon. She even saw Vince and his gang huddled together away from the crowd, by the rocks that jutted into the water.

How did all these kids find out about this party? Karen wondered. Somehow word had gotten out, and everyone for fifty miles had shown up at the cove, ready to party.

The cove was such a beautiful place to snorkel. It was protected by rock jetties on two sides so that the water stayed clear and calm.

Karen couldn't wait to put on the mask and fins and try snorkeling again. Her first experience had been horrifying. She knew she had to snorkel again to get it behind her.

If only Jerry wouldn't be such a worried mother hen. He'd been acting that way ever since two days before when she had told him about how her shoulder had been burned and showed him her bandaged hand and shoulder. A look of horror had frozen on his face when she told him. He hadn't said a word, just stared at her in disbelief.

After telling him about the suntan lotion, she decided she might as well tell him everything that had been happening. There was no reason to keep it from him. She probably should have told him sooner.

They were sitting on Venice Beach, shaded by a large yellow beach umbrella. She leaned against him, her back against his side, and told him about how someone was trying to keep her away from him. At first, she admitted, she had suspected Renee. She had even suspected Renee of trying to murder her on the rocks.

But someone else was trying to murder her. It was clear. Most likely, it was the girl pretending to be Jerry's sister.

She couldn't see Jerry's face, but she could tell

by the way his muscles tensed that he was very upset by what she was telling him. Finally she turned and stared into his eyes. "Do you have any idea who is doing it, who is trying to keep me away from you?"

His face went blank. His eyes seemed to die. Karen thought she saw real sadness in his eyes. But the sadness faded, too. "I'm really sorry this is happening," he said finally.

"But who *is* it?" she insisted.

"I don't know. I'm just so . . . shocked. I had no idea this was happening to you. I'm just so . . . sorry."

For a brief moment, she was sorry she had told him. He seemed even more upset about it than she did.

But he had to know.

He had to help her.

"You've got to help me find out who it is," she had said.

"Of course." He had put his arm around her. They hadn't talked about it again.

Now, two days later, her shoulder feeling better, she was about to go snorkeling in the cove with him. "We won't go out too far," he said, as they pulled on their fins at the edge of the shore. "In case your shoulder gets tired."

"Please, Jerry — stop worrying about me," Karen snapped. He really was getting on her nerves. "I'll go out by myself if you don't shut up. I really will."

He looked hurt. She realized she was nervous

about going snorkeling again and was just taking it out on him. She apologized quickly, putting a hand on his shoulder.

He smiled. "Ready?"

She spit into her mask and rubbed the saliva around the glass. "Ready." Before pulling on the mask, she looked back at the crowded beach, searching for Ann-Marie. She shouldn't be hard to find, Karen thought. She was wearing a Day-Glo green bikini.

But Ann-Marie wasn't back on their blanket. Karen couldn't find her anywhere. She's probably sneaked off with Mike, Karen thought.

Every time she thought of Mike and Ann-Marie together, it gave Karen a laugh.

"Come on. Let's go see what's out there," Jerry called, already several steps ahead of her. Karen pulled on her mask, adjusted it, pulled the mouthpiece into her mouth, and followed him into the clear, blue-green water.

The water of the cove was shallow for only a few yards. Then the bottom dipped drastically and the water became deep and even more clear. It's so beautiful here, Karen thought, floating forward, breathing steadily through the snorkel, kicking the fins slowly behind her.

Jerry was floating right ahead of her. She pulled back to avoid bumping into his pedaling fins. She stared down at the secret, blue-green world beneath her. Dozens of silvery fish swam past, ignoring her.

I feel like a visitor to another planet, she thought.

When she raised her head above the surface to

find Jerry, she saw that they had floated out a lot further than she'd imagined. "The current — it's taking us straight out!" she shouted.

Jerry, several yards ahead of her, raised his head and let some water out of his mask. "What?"

"I said the current is taking us out," Karen repeated.

She wasn't sure if he heard her this time or not. "How's your shoulder?" he called.

"It's okay, I guess." Actually, it ached a little. "What?"

She floated closer so he could hear her. "We shouldn't go out too far," she repeated. "It's the current," she said. "It's deceptive. The water looks perfectly calm, but there's a real pull."

"There's so much to see." He fiddled with his snorkel. "There's a reef right out there," he said, pointing, "with some really amazing formations."

He slipped his mask back on, blew some water out of the air hose, and headed straight out toward the reef. Karen, a little reluctant because of her shoulder, watched him. He's such a strong, confident swimmer, she thought. He really is like a sleek fish in the water.

Impulsively, she flattened out over the water and floated after him. Holding her arms low at her sides kept her shoulder from hurting. But now her burned hand was throbbing with pain.

Maybe this wasn't such a good idea after all, she thought. Maybe I should've waited a few more days.

But it was so beautiful down there; slender, silent fish were slithering through shafts of cloudy yellow light. She floated further, listening to her breathing, alone, alone in this new world of swimming colors.

Where was the reef Jerry had pointed to? She couldn't see it. The ocean floor seemed to drop once again.

Had she gotten turned around?

She raised her head out of the water, pulling down the mask. "Jerry?"

She didn't see him at first. It took a while for her eyes to adjust to the brightness. "Jerry?"

There he was, several yards up ahead.

She looked back at the beach, so far away.

Too far.

Her shoulder ached now. Her hand throbbed with pain. "Jerry?"

She had gone too far out. Normally, she would have been able to swim back. But now she was in too much pain. Jerry would have to help her.

"Jerry?"

Finally he raised his head and spun around, searching for her. "You okay?" he smiled, then pulled down the mask, letting it hang down over his neck.

She had been feeling a little panicky, but his smile reassured her. He swam back to her, with long, sure strokes that cut through the current.

He looked so sweet, so concerned, she impulsively leaped up and kissed him. After a few seconds, he pulled away. His expression had changed. "Why'd you do that?" he asked.

"Uh . . . I was thanking you in advance," Karen said, surprised by the coldness of the question. "I think you have to help me get back."

He frowned. "Your shoulder?"

"And my hand. I guess this was stupid." She put a hand on the shoulder of his wet suit. "Take me back?"

"But we just got here." His anger startled her.

"Really. I'm sorry, but I can't swim back by myself. I need your help."

"I can't help you," he said.

Something about the way he looked at her gave her a chill. His face grew hard, his eyes as clear and cold as the water.

"What did you say?"

"I can't help you."

Why was he staring at her like that, so coldly, as if he didn't know her, as if he didn't like her?

"Jerry, did you hear me?" She couldn't keep the panic from her voice. "I need your help to get back."

"I'm not Jerry," he said, staring hard, not blinking. "I'm Todd."

Chapter 21

"Jerry — stop it!" Was this some kind of a joke?

His cold expression didn't change. "Jerry's gone." Even his voice sounded harder, colder. He still hadn't blinked.

"Jerry, that's enough."

"I told you — I'm Todd."

"Please — help me! My shoulder hurts. I can't stay here. You've got to help me." She suddenly felt sick. The bobbing up and down, the beach so far away, the chill of the water, the throbbing of her shoulder — none of it was as frightening as the look on Jerry's face.

"Jerry hasn't been the same since I died," he said.

"What? What are you talking about?"

It wasn't a joke. There was something seriously wrong with him. What could she do? How could she snap him out of it?

"Ever since I drowned, Jerry hasn't been quite right. Know what I mean?" He didn't wait for an answer. "It was Jerry's fault that I drowned. He knew he could have saved me. I knew it, too. That's why I keep doing this to Jerry."

"Doing what?" Karen asked, not recognizing her trembling voice, staring hard into Jerry's frozen eyes, unable to look away.

"That's why I keep coming back. To warn people."

"To warn people?"

"Yes." He pulled back his lips in an eerie, terrifying smile. "I keep coming back to warn people to stay away from Jerry."

Karen cried out in shock. She choked on a mouthful of water. Finally she sputtered, "It was *you*?!"

"I tried to warn you. It wasn't easy. Jerry doesn't like it when I take over his body like this."

"*You* were warning me against *yourself*?"

"I warned you to stay away from Jerry. I warned Renee, too, but she didn't listen. So I had to do something *bad* to Renee."

"No!" Karen cried. "No! No! No!" She forced herself to look away from those cold, unblinking eyes.

How could this be Jerry? He seemed so sweet, so . . . nice.

She turned and started to swim away from him. The beach was a ribbon of yellow in the distance. She was too far from shore to scream for help. Too far . . . to swim back. The current was pulling her back. Her entire right side throbbed with pain.

I'm not going to make it, she realized.

And then he grabbed her by her bad shoulder,

and turned her around. "Let go of me!" she screamed.

He shoved her hard. She cried out from the pain.

"I warned you, Karen. I warned you about Jerry. Jerry is bad. Jerry let me drown."

"Stop, please — " She struggled to get away from him, but her arm hurt too much. She couldn't swim. She couldn't think straight because of the pain. She couldn't escape.

"Jerry is bad," he said. "Jerry has to be punished."

"Please, please, please!"

"Too late for please, Karen. Too late for you. Too late for me. Too late for Jerry. Jerry is bad."

With startling quickness, he grabbed her snorkeling mask with one hand, pulled it off, and tossed it away. Then he dived beneath the surface. A few seconds later he reappeared, swimming to shore with strong, steady strokes.

He swam nearly halfway back before he turned around. When he looked back, Karen had stopped her struggles to stay afloat.

He watched her go under. She didn't come back up.

I warned her, he thought. I did my best to warn her.

He continued swimming back to shore.

Chapter 22

Her right side throbbing, Karen did a surface dive down into the water.

"I'm not Jerry. I'm Todd." The words repeated and repeated in her ears. *"Jerry is bad."*

She opened her eyes and forced herself down, holding her breath. The salt water stung, but she could see clearly.

There it was. She reached out, kicked hard twice with her fins, and pulled the snorkeling mask in with her good hand.

Holding it tightly, she burst up to the surface, gasping for air.

If I snorkel back, I think I can make it, she thought, straightening the mouthpiece and clearing the air hose of water. It will take a while against the current. But it's my only hope.

If she snorkeled, she realized, she wouldn't have to use her arms. She could keep her throbbing, aching arm down at her side and, breathing with her head under the surface, propel herself by kicking the fins.

That's probably why Jerry tossed away her mask. He didn't want her floating back, able to take her time and breathe as she made her way.

Poor, crazy Jerry.

Bringing back Todd the only way he knew how.

Punishing himself again and again for Todd's death.

Poor, crazy Jerry. Poor, crazy Jerry.

She kept up the refrain, repeating it in rhythm, as she kicked and breathed, kicked and breathed, not seeing anything now but a blur of blues and greens, pushing against the current, forcing her way back to the beach.

It seemed like hours later that she stood up in the shallow water near the shore and stumbled toward the sand, pulling down the hood of the wet suit, breathing so hard, her legs like jelly, her chest feeling about to burst.

"Hey — Karen!"

She shielded her eyes from the lowering yellow sun. Who was it?

"Karen — you okay?"

"Vince — is that you?" She was still too dizzy, too out-of-breath to talk.

He ran up to her in his cutoffs and sleeveless blue T-shirt, and she slumped against him, holding herself up by putting an arm around his shoulder.

"Vince, how did you know . . . ?"

"I saw Jerry come back. But I didn't see you." He put a strong arm around her waist and led her up onto dry sand.

"Jerry? Where is he? We've got to stop him."

"What?"

"He's crazy, Vince. He's very sick. He tried to kill me."

"Okay, okay. Calm down, Karen," he said softly, helping her walk. "First, let's take care of you. Then — "

"NO!" Karen shrieked, seeing the tall, red-haired girl running toward her.

Vince was so startled by her scream, he let go of her.

Karen took a few uncertain steps back. This girl who claimed to be Jerry's sister — she had threatened Karen before. What did she want now? Why was she following her?

"What are *you* doing here?" Karen screamed as the girl came running up, looking flushed, and desperate.

"Where's Jerry? Have you seen him?" she asked.

"He tried to kill me," Karen blurted out. "Who are you? Why are you here? Why are you following me?"

"I've been trying to tell you," the girl said, her eyes searching the crowded beach. "I'm Jerry's sister. I knew Jerry was sick — but I didn't know how sick. You've got to believe me."

"Jerry said he doesn't have a sister," Karen replied skeptically.

"Yes," the girl said sadly, still searching the beach. "Ever since Todd died, Jerry has been so confused, so guilty. He closed the rest of us out. He's pretended I don't exist. It was as if he only had room for Todd. I've been trying to get help for him, but it's been impossible. He just — "

"There he goes!" Karen interrupted, pointing.

Several yards up the beach, beside the now deserted volleyball net, Jerry turned and saw them.

"Get him!" Jerry's sister cried. "Please — before he does something awful!"

Chapter 23

Vince took off, his bare feet kicking up sand as he ran.

"Get him! Please — don't let Jerry run away!" Jerry's sister cried, running after Vince.

Karen stood frozen on the spot.

"I'm not Jerry. I'm Todd."

She heard the hard, cold voice once again. Then, shaking her head hard, as if trying to drive the sounds from her mind, she started running toward Jerry, too.

What will he do if we catch him? Karen wondered. She thought of poor Renee. Renee had trusted Jerry. Renee had been with Jerry through the bad times after Todd's death. Did she have any idea how sick Jerry was?

Did she have any idea that sometimes Jerry thought he was Todd? Had Todd terrorized Renee, too, the way he terrorized Karen?

The morning Jerry killed her, did Renee have any idea why?

To Karen's surprise, Jerry made no attempt to

run from Vince. He stood there on the sand by the volleyball net, watching the three of them approach.

And then he started to run *to* them.

"Hi!" he called, a cheerful smile on his face.

Karen realized he was smiling at *her*.

"Karen — hi! How's the shoulder? Feel okay?"

Jerry started to run right past Vince, but Vince grabbed him around the chest and held on. "Hey — what's going on?" Jerry protested, but without any real anger.

"It's going to be okay, Jerry," his sister said softly.

Jerry looked at her as if he didn't recognize her. "Karen, how was the snorkeling?" he asked.

Karen stared into his eyes. They were alive and warm again.

"It was okay," she said quietly.

"I'll take him," Jerry's sister said to Vince.

Vince let go reluctantly. "You sure?"

Jerry made no attempt to run. "Come with me, Jerry. I'm going to get you help." His sister took his hand and started to lead him away. Jerry allowed her to pull him, having to hurry to stay with her.

After they were halfway to the parking lot, Jerry turned back and called to Karen, "See you later. I'll call you, okay?"

"Okay," Karen said, tears welling up in her eyes.

Poor, crazy Jerry.

He was going off with his sister so willingly.

He *wanted* to be stopped. He *wanted* to be helped.

He had tried to let her know from the night that he had met her.

Stay away from Jerry.

That was his desperate message, his plea to her. He tried to tell her. She just wouldn't listen.

Without realizing it, she was leaning against Vince again as they made their way to get her belongings, and he had his arm securely around her waist.

"Hey," she said, stopping. "Are you really someone I can lean on?"

He laughed.

"You don't *look* like someone I can lean on," she teased.

"Try me," he said. He scooped her off her feet and carried her across the sand.

About the Author

R.L. STINE is the author of more than sixty books of horror, humor, and adventure for young people, and was formerly a magazine editor at Scholastic. He lives and works in New York City with his wife, Jane, and his son, Matthew. Lately most of his energy has gone into writing scary novels for teenage readers.

point®

Other books you will enjoy,
about real kids like you!

point ® **THRILLERS**

☐ MC44330-5	**The Accident** Diane Hoh	$2.95
☐ MC43115-3	**April Fools** Richie Tankersley Cusick	$2.95
☐ MC44236-8	**The Baby-sitter** R.L. Stine	$3.25
☐ MC44332-1	**The Baby-sitter II** R.L. Stine	$3.25
☐ MC43278-8	**Beach Party** R.L. Stine	$2.95
☐ MC43125-0	**Blind Date** R.L. Stine	$3.25
☐ MC43279-6	**The Boyfriend** R.L. Stine	$3.25
☐ MC44316-X	**The Cheerleader** Caroline B. Cooney	$2.95
☐ MC45401-3	**The Fever** Diane Hoh	$3.25
☐ MC43291-5	**Final Exam** A. Bates	$2.95
☐ MC41641-3	**The Fire** Caroline B. Cooney	$2.95
☐ MC43806-9	**The Fog** Caroline B. Cooney	$2.95
☐ MC43050-5	**Funhouse** Diane Hoh	$3.25
☐ MC44333-X	**The Girlfriend** R.L. Stine	$3.25
☐ MC45385-8	**Hit and Run** R.L. Stine	$3.25
☐ MC44904-4	**The Invitation** Diane Hoh	$2.95
☐ MC43203-6	**The Lifeguard** Richie Tankersley Cusick	$2.95
☐ MC45246-0	**Mirror, Mirror** D.E. Athkins	$3.25
☐ MC44582-0	**Mother's Helper** A. Bates	$2.95
☐ MC44768-8	**My Secret Admirer** Carol Ellis	$2.95
☐ MC44238-4	**Party Line** A. Bates	$2.95
☐ MC44237-6	**Prom Dress** Lael Littke	$2.95
☐ MC44884-6	**The Return of the Vampire** Caroline B. Cooney	$2.95
☐ MC44941-9	**Sister Dearest** D.E. Athkins	$2.95
☐ MC43014-9	**Slumber Party** Christopher Pike	$3.25
☐ MC41640-5	**The Snow** Caroline B. Cooney	$3.25
☐ MC43280-X	**The Snowman** R.L. Stine	$3.25
☐ MC43114-5	**Teacher's Pet** Richie Tankersley Cusick	$2.95
☐ MC43742-9	**Thirteen** Edited by T. Pines	$3.50
☐ MC44235-X	**Trick or Treat** Richie Tankersley Cusick	$2.95
☐ MC43139-0	**Twisted** R.L. Stine	$3.25
☐ MC45063-8	**The Waitress** Sinclair Smith	$2.95
☐ MC44256-2	**Weekend** Christopher Pike	$2.95
☐ MC44916-8	**The Window** Carol Ellis	$2.95

Available wherever you buy books, or use this order form.

Scholastic Inc., P.O. Box 7502, 2931 East McCarty Street, Jefferson City, MO 65102

Please send me the books I have checked above. I am enclosing $_____ (please add
$2.00 to cover shipping and handling). Send check or money order — no cash or C.O.D.s please.

Name _____

Address_____

City_____ State/Zip_____
Please allow four to six weeks for delivery Offer good in the U.S. only Sorry, mail orders are not
available to residents of Canada. Prices subject to change.   PT991